SEE YOU DOWN THE ROAD

Kim Ablon Whitney

For Matt

Published by
Dell Laurel-Leaf
an imprint of
Random House Children's Books
a division of Random House, Inc.
New York

Visit us on the Web! www.randomhouse.com/teens

Educators and librarians, for a variety of teaching tools, visit us at www.randomhouse.com/teachers

ISBN: 0-440-23809-9

RL: 7.5

Reprinted by arrangement with Alfred A. Knopf Books for Young Readers

Printed in the United States of America

First Dell Laurel-Leaf Edition July 2005

10 9 8 7 6 5 4 3 2 1

OPM

There ain't no surer way to find out whether you like people or hate them than to travel with them.

—Mark Twain

chapter 1

One good thing about living in a trailer is that you don't have to pack when you leave town. You just go.

We took off for the summer before it was really even spring, before Florida thinned out to just the people who actually live there year round. I knew we weren't staying in Miami all year since we never do, but I also didn't know we were leaving until Jimmy and Patrick came into the store.

I was working the afternoon alone while Mrs. C. was out seeing some artsy-craftsy dealer about his overpriced knick-knacks tourists shit their pants over. Jimmy and Patrick came in, and at first I thought they were customers, so I stubbed out my butt and stashed the Coke can I was tapping my ashes into and the book I was reading under the counter. When I saw it was just them, I took the ashtray back out and relit my cigarette but left the book where it was.

"Working hard or hardly working?" Jimmy said with that cocky grin he had all the time. Ever since he'd turned eighteen, he walked around like he could do anything he wanted. Dad said what he needed was a good beating to set him straight, and I was starting to agree.

"What do you want?" There was no way Jimmy stopped by just to say hey. Patrick—maybe. Jimmy—no way. Even though Jimmy and I were only two years apart, we'd never been close.

Jimmy shrugged. "Can't I just stop by to see my little sister?"

"No. So tell me what you want."

Jimmy shifted his gaze to the back of the store where Mrs. C. had her office. "I don't think your little *Country* boss would like you smoking on the job."

Even though all of us Travelers called people who weren't Travelers Country folk or Country people, the way Jimmy said *Country* it sounded like an insult.

Usually I snuck one or two cigarettes when Mrs. C. was out and then sprayed air freshener since smoking wasn't allowed in the store. "She's not here," I told Jimmy, and wished I hadn't when he smirked and said, "Well, then, I'm gonna need a few things since we're heading off."

And that's when I knew we were leaving—nice that Mom and Dad hadn't bothered to tell me.

Jimmy swaggered to the men's section, fingering this shirt and touching that shirt. Patrick came to the counter and stared at me with those eyes of his that are so pale, they're more white than blue. My insides twisted, and I wished for a second that he wasn't so damn good-looking.

"You go to school this week?" he asked.

"A few days."

"I swear you're the only person I know who actually likes school."

"Who says I like school?"

"You *go*."

I shrugged. "There's nothing better to do."

This was a lame excuse for why I kept going when every other Traveler quit right after they could read, write, and do simple math—after they'd learned all that school could teach them that would be of any use in our world. But I kind of got off on some school stuff, like my paper on the Black Sox baseball scandal of 1919, which now I wouldn't be finishing. But if I told anyone that—Patrick, Jimmy, Ann, Mom, Dad—they'd think I was crazy. They already wondered about me.

"You guys staying around longer?" I asked Patrick.

He rested his forearms on the counter, leaned toward me, and smiled. Even though he'd never had braces, had hardly ever been to the dentist unless something was really wrong—none of us had—his teeth lined up perfectly. It wasn't the only thing about Patrick's looks that was near perfect. There was his smooth skin that freckled just slightly in the summer and his brown hair that fell onto his forehead whenever he broke a sweat.

"We're going with you," he said.

Another minor detail Mom and Dad hadn't bothered to fill me in on. I swallowed and found there was a sudden lump in my throat. Not because we were traveling with the Murphys, but because of what that meant. It meant it wouldn't be long before Patrick and I were married.

"Hey, Pat," Jimmy called. "Come here."

Patrick walked to where Jimmy was modeling one of the most expensive items in the store—a blue Tommy Hilfiger jacket. He was checking himself out in the full-length mirror, thinking he was some kind of hot shit. I marched over and told him to take it off.

3

"What're you gonna do if I don't?" he said, loving every minute of torturing me.

"Jimmy, stop being such an asshole."

"That's nice language, Bridget. Real nice."

Jimmy ripped the tag off the jacket sleeve and handed it to me. I can't believe I was so stupid as to just take it from him. What I should have done was tell him to shove it straight up his ass.

"See ya later," he said. Patrick followed him out the door, not saying anything because he couldn't or he'd look like a loser in front of Jimmy. I couldn't blame him. On the way out, Jimmy grabbed a pair of sunglasses and a baseball hat. Total including the jacket: over two hundred dollars.

After they left, my mind whirled as I tried to figure out what to do. I had just about two hundred dollars buried underneath the back wheel of the trailer, but there was no way I was spending my hard-earned money on Jimmy's clothes. Squealing on Jimmy to Mom and Dad wasn't worth thinking about for more than a second, since being a snitch was worse than anything for a Traveler. I knew most Travelers would just walk out right then and there, forgetting all about Mrs. C. and the store. But most Travelers wouldn't be working a Country job to begin with.

Mrs. C. came back a lot earlier than she said she was going to, and I was still figuring things out. Besides knocking over the Coke can and spilling ashes on the floor as I tried to stash it under the counter, I'd left the price tag to the jacket out. When she saw the tag, she thought I'd sold it.

"Oh, Bridget, you made such a great sale!"

Her smile disappeared when I told her that I hadn't sold it. She took off her huge floppy straw hat that was practically bigger than she was and started fingering the edges of it as I told the story. I said four Hispanic townies from South Beach had come in and tried on some stuff, and one of them had the jacket on, and I was ringing him up and treating him just like any other customer because that's what Mrs. C. had always taught me to do—treat anybody and everybody like the best customer. I knew making them Hispanic would get her on my side. I said he asked me to take the tag off so he could wear the jacket out. But then when I did, another one threw something at me—a Coke can full of ashes, I think—and they all ran out. Of course I tried to run after them, but I had the stuff flying in my eyes and by the time I . . .

Mrs. C. said she was just glad I was okay. I thought that would be that. Even though she complained about hard times and how the store wasn't doing so well since the Target had moved in next door, she had to have plenty of cash from her husband's life insurance policy. I figured she'd just dig into her funds or whatever and lick her wounds and no big deal. But she dialed 911, saying, "You got a good look at them, right? We can't let people like that get away with this."

We waited around until this crater-faced pig, Officer Ligatari, showed up, and at first he bought my story just like Mrs. C. Then he asked for my address and phone number to file the report, and when I told him I lived over at the trailer park, he freaked out. Up until then he'd thought I was just a regular kid, which is what most people thought about me. All of us Travelers fit in well—we had to in order to do what we did. We were good at being just like everybody else—except when it came to a few important things. Like how we made our money.

Officer Ligatari eyed me suspiciously. "Trailer park? And you didn't know these townies?" He didn't know I was a

Traveler. If he knew about us, like some of the cops did, that would have been enough to cuff me right away. What he did know was that anybody living in a trailer park was no good.

I shook my head. "Never saw them before in my life."

"Were they smoking when they came in?"

Mrs. C. piped up. "We don't allow smoking in the store."

Ligatari didn't take his eyes off me. "Were they smoking when they came in the store, Bridget?"

I hadn't had time for the air freshener and I'd already started with the bit about the ashes. "One was. I asked him to put it out."

"And he didn't?"

"No."

"Why didn't you ask him to leave?"

"Because he was about to buy the jacket and we haven't exactly been making many sales lately."

Ligatari nodded like he had it all figured out. "Maybe," he said. "But maybe they were friends of yours? Could that possibly be the case?"

"I told you I never saw them before. They were townies."

There was a moment when we were all silent. Ligatari was probably thinking I was some first-timer about to crack and dissolve into a pool of guilty tears, admitting everything. I wasn't sure what Mrs. C. was thinking. Maybe she was wondering whether I *did* know them. Whether I *had* set it up.

But then she slung her arm around my shoulders and I got a whiff of the lavender perfume she always wore. "Look," she told Ligatari, "Bridget didn't know them. Now can you do anything based on the descriptions she gave you?"

Of course he said he couldn't do much unless they happened to rip off another store in the neighborhood and got caught. Ligatari eyed me one more time. "But I don't think that's going to happen in this case. I don't think this was a case of those boys just walking into this store at random."

That night at dinner I tried to forget about Mrs. C. When I didn't show up for work Monday and there was no trace of us left in all of Miami, maybe she'd call Ligatari and he'd say I told you so. But it didn't matter. By then we'd be hundreds of miles away.

Mom loved to cook and was always reading cooking magazines. She'd study the pictures and the recipes, but she hardly ever made any of them because Dad only liked meals with one-word names like chicken or steak. The few times she'd broken down and tried something small, like special sauce, Dad would take a bite, swallow like he'd just eaten dirt, and say something like "What is this garbage?" which would stop Mom from trying anything different for another long while.

All four of us were at the kitchen table, and the TV was on so loud you wouldn't think we'd be able to talk over it. But pretty soon, I couldn't hear the TV at all. All I could hear was Mom, Dad, and Jimmy.

"That's too much," Dad said, stabbing one of the slices of meat loaf Mom had put on Jimmy's plate with his fork and sliding it onto my plate instead.

Heaviness ran in our family—or on Dad's side of the family—and Dad worried Jimmy was losing his boyish look, which was important for what we did. If you were a young, decent-looking kid, it was amazing how much you could get away with. Jimmy had thickened up over the past few years. He'd put on at least thirty pounds, but luckily he'd sprouted a few more

7

inches too. Now he stood just over six feet and was what people down south called well fed.

Jimmy stared back at Dad. "Look who's talking."

Jimmy did have a point. Dad's face was thin, but he kept punching holes in his belt. Dad warned, "Jimmy, watch it."

But Jimmy didn't, of course.

"So what's the plan? We pick up a trailer, sell it, then what?"

"I figure we start roofing and then maybe do a bit of barn painting."

Jimmy scoffed. "Roofing? Painting? Come on, Dad, that's for hacks."

Dad locked his jaw and spoke with his mouth almost shut. It was how he'd spoken when I'd told him I wanted to keep going to school and that I was getting a Country job. Dad claimed I had to drop out because Mom needed me working jobs with her. But Mom was the one who said she wanted me to get as much of an education as I could before I married, and she was the one who paid for me to go to St. Jude's. Dad said paying for an education was crazy and he wasn't doing it, but Mom knew that if we went to public school our education would be even shorter since if you left before the school year was up or started late, which we always did, they'd report you to social services. The nuns at St. Jude's knew who we were and understood our ways enough to know there was no changing things. Anyway, the real reason Dad didn't want me going to school was because he didn't want me hanging out with Country folk any more than I had to. He also worried that no self-respecting Traveler boy would want to marry a girl with more of an education than him. But I already had a few years more schooling than Patrick and it didn't seem to bother him.

Dad stared at Jimmy. "There ain't nothing wrong with roofing and painting. It makes a fine living, has for our people for years."

"But it's not big money," Jimmy snapped back.

"Big money'll get you prison. That where you want to be— do some time, like your uncle?"

This was enough to get Mom going. She whined, "What good's a bunch of money in prison, Jimmy?"

"It's better than no money sitting around roofing. At least Big Jim's doing something real."

Dad clanked down his fork and knife. Talking down roofing and painting was bad, but talking up our uncle, Big Jim, was worse. From Dad's reddening face I was sure he was about to give Jimmy that beating and I'd have a ringside seat. But then Dad said with a smirk, "I'll tell you what. You settle down this summer, and if roofing and painting don't do it, then maybe getting you engaged will." Dad knew the idea of getting married and settling down into a life of everyday scams scared Jimmy worse than any beating.

Jimmy jumped up from the table, kicked over his chair, and bolted out the door. Dad went after him as far as a few steps out the door, screaming, "Get back here!" But Jimmy was gone.

Later that night, when Mom and Dad were asleep, someone whispered my name outside my window. I was still up reading *Eight Men Out*, one of the books I'd found at the library for my Black Sox paper. I didn't know why I was still reading it since we were leaving in a few days and we wouldn't be back until the fall. But I couldn't stop. I loved to read—something everyone else thought was just plain strange—but more than anything I loved reading true stories. It was different than reading other stuff that maybe you could sit around and talk about but then in the end you always came back to the same thing: that it was just someone's imagination, not real life. I liked reading things that had actually happened—stories that you couldn't just put behind you when you turned the last page.

I thought it might be Jimmy outside—he still hadn't come back. I tiptoed out the trailer door, easing it closed. When I didn't see anyone, I crept to the other side of the trailer. That's when Patrick grabbed me from behind and at the same time covered my mouth with his hand, which was good because otherwise I'd have woken Mom and Dad.

"Patrick, Jesus," I whispered when he took his hand away. I was about to tell him he had scared the shit out of me, but then he leaned close and kissed me. The first time I'd ever kissed Patrick was only a few months before at my cousin's wedding. That was right after our parents announced our engagement. Before that everybody knew our parents were planning for us to get married, so it was always like "Bridget and Patrick." But we'd never kissed. Then at the wedding, it wasn't a real deep kiss. Tonight though, our kissing was deep. Patrick kissed me hard. It was kind of cool to be kissed like that. Like he wanted me. The force of his lips against mine made me press back harder, surprising myself.

Patrick tasted like beer, and I asked him if he'd been out with Jimmy. He said they'd been out at some bar. Patrick hadn't heard about the fight with Dad, though, beyond Jimmy saying Dad was a *kull*, which was Cant—old Traveler language—for idiot, so I filled him in.

"What's wrong with him?" I asked. "Why's he acting so crazy?"

Patrick shrugged.

"You're his best friend."

"Jimmy's just being Jimmy."

"Yeah, an asshole."

Patrick smiled at the word *asshole*. He liked that I was tough. "I heard you handled the pigs real good today," he said.

"How'd you hear that?"

"How do you think? Ann."

I hadn't told Ann—who's my best friend and also happens to be Patrick's younger sister—not to tell Patrick, so I can't be mad at her.

"Did you tell Jimmy?"

"Nah."

"Good. He'd just think it was funny, me getting in trouble because of him. I can't believe I'm gonna have to deal with his shit all summer."

Patrick leaned close again, so close that I smelled the aftershave he wore to cover up the smell of tar that he couldn't get rid of from working driveways and roofs. "Forget about Jimmy. This summer's gonna be cool."

I knew he was talking about more than us traveling together, more than just the summer. We'd never really talked about it straight out—about us getting married. I guess because it had always seemed a ways off. But if everyone got along this summer, they'd set a date. I knew that shouldn't scare me, but it did. It wasn't that Patrick wasn't nice or cute. He was both and more. But marriage? Even just the word sent shivers through me. *Marriage.* It seemed so final, so fixed.

"You sure?" I asked.

"Yeah."

Patrick held me close again, and we stood outside the trailer in the dark with the smell of the orange blossoms all around us, kissing. I felt like we could stay there kissing forever, but finally Patrick pulled away.

"You better get back," he sighed.

"Yeah."

He kissed me once more, this time on the top of my head. "See you tomorrow."

I crept back inside the trailer, took out my book, and tried reading again, but all I kept thinking was, *What did it matter anymore?* School was behind me, at least for the summer. And I probably wouldn't go back in the fall either, since by then the date for the wedding would be set. Mom and Dad would say I shouldn't be thinking about school but about getting married. I closed my eyes and tried to remember kissing Patrick, but all I could hear in my head was that word again, the *M* word. I wished I didn't think of Patrick and immediately think of marriage. Why couldn't I just think of his tongue touching mine, the rush of being so close to him? But Patrick meant marriage, and that meant all the stuff that went with it—our own trailer, making dinner for him after long days working, probably even kids. When I was younger all that had seemed so cool—having a husband and your own trailer. It was all us girls talked about. But that was when it had been far away, something I'd be ready for when the time came. Only now the time was here, and I didn't feel anything close to ready.

chapter 2

We left Miami a few days later and spent a night in Georgia, then headed through Tennessee to Kentucky, where we bought another trailer and towed it back on Jimmy's hitch through North Carolina to South Carolina.

It'd only been a few days on the road, but it felt like weeks. Even after months of not traveling, it was easy to fall back into it. To get used to the slow lurch of the trailer, the hum of the engine, the whoosh of the air rushing by, the smell of Dad's stale coffee, the black asphalt falling away behind us and stretching out endlessly in front of us.

We settled in for what Dad expected would be a few days at a campground called the Traveler's Pause. We could never be sure how long we'd stay in one place—it always depended on how the work was and whether someone got suspicious of us. We always had to be ready to leave on a moment's notice.

The Traveler's Pause was a big campground, and all kinds of people passed through it, not just Travelers. There was also a section with people who had made the campground their permanent home. The Pause was right near the highway, and no matter where you were, you could hear the traffic whizzing by.

We parked our trailer on one part of the grounds and the one we'd bought from the dealer in Kentucky on another part. Luckily Jimmy stayed in the one we were selling and I stayed with Mom and Dad in ours, so I didn't have to put up with him. "You better not mess it up," Mom warned Jimmy. "You hear me?"

Selling the trailers was Mom's thing, and I helped her with it. She put an ad in the local paper, and right after it came out, a couple came to see it. Mom told them to come to our trailer first, and I crawled under a blanket on the couch and looked as sick as I could. After years of doing it, I was crazy good at it. I messed up my hair and wet it near my forehead so I looked like I was feverish, and then I lay back and sort of twisted around, but not so much that it looked fake.

When the couple showed up, Mom let them in but immediately shushed them and pointed to me. Then she led them outside and my job was over. I threw off the blanket and peeked at them through the window.

They were the usual type. Sixtyish, gray-haired couple, she mildly overweight so her face blended into her body without a neck, and he skinny with a bad comb-over. Just by looking at them, I knew their whole story. Now that their kids were grown and they'd retired, they wanted to live, to travel and see the country, if they couldn't see the world. But hotels or even motels were too expensive, and who wanted to sleep in a different bed and eat out every night anyway? They wanted to travel yet have some of the comforts of home. He wanted to watch the ball game in the afternoon, for Chrissake! So, the perfect solution: an RV. Then they saw the ad and couldn't believe the price. . . .

"Is she okay?" the woman asked Mom outside.

Mom shook her head like I'd seen her do a million times before and looked at the ground all depressed. Then, bringing her eyes up again, she pretended very convincingly to hold back tears. It helped that Mom was little and pretty and people didn't like to see a pretty little woman cry. Mom was the only one of us Daughertys who wasn't that tall. Even in her going-out heels, she stood only five four, and she was thin too. Jimmy definitely had Dad's genes. I wasn't sure yet about myself, whether I was stuck with Dad's or got lucky and had Mom's. I was already taller than Mom by a few inches, which wasn't a good sign. But I had Mom's hazel eyes and light brown hair, and that gave me hope. If I never grew another inch I'd be happy. The only thing I wanted to keep growing was my hair, which stretched halfway down my back. I didn't wear it down that much, but I liked it long because I could do so much with it—braid it, put it in a ponytail or pigtails, or clip it up on top of my head.

"She's real sick," Mom said, sniffling. "Nothing we can do now but just wait and pray."

"Sick?"

Mom whispered the word *cancer* like it pained her just to say it. "That's why we gotta sell the trailer, actually. It was for her and her husband-to-be. A weddin' present. But now there'll be no weddin'. And we need the money—you know, medical expenses and all."

"I am *so* sorry," the woman said.

Mom heaved a sigh and looked like she was on the verge of tears again. If Mom needed to, she could actually cry on command. "Come on, I'll show you the trailer. I put it over on the other side of the campground so she wouldn't have to see it out the window. See what her life was gonna be—what she'll never have now—if you know what I mean."

"Of course. Of course we do."

When Mom came back she said she'd no doubt hooked the woman but the husband still couldn't believe we'd be unloading that nice a trailer for only $17,250. I could hear Mom's voice in my head as she told me. *I know, it's a crime really, giving this trailer away for practically half price, it being new and all. I hate to have to do it, but we just need the money so badly now.* The truth was the trailer had only cost Mom and Dad $11,000 because the manufacturer was discontinuing the line. He needed to get rid of them cheap, so he'd sell to just about anybody, even us, when he knew perfectly well who we were and what we did. And since it was illegal for him to sell to us because we weren't licensed dealers, we could be sure he wouldn't go telling.

Mom wagged her finger at me. "Give her a few hours. She'll get him to come around. Men are always more skeptical—you remember that, Bridget. But when they fall, they fall harder than women."

When the couple left I went to find Ann. She was sitting on the steps of the Murphys' trailer, scribbling in the spiral-bound notebook she always had with her.

"Hey, girl," she said as she finished jotting. "Listen to this." Ann read from what she'd just written. "He pressed close to her, and she could feel him then. She could feel the power of his manliness throbbing." Ann looked up at me. "Isn't that good? I mean, isn't that a good name for it—'the power of his manliness'?"

I tried not to laugh or even smile. "Definitely." Ann was serious when it came to her writing. When Jimmy told her she was never going to be able to write a whole book—even a book of romance trash—and sell it for the millions she imagined, she didn't talk to him for a week, which was saying something given the way Ann felt about Jimmy.

I plopped down next to her. She pulled out her pack of cigarettes and handed me one.

"What's up?" I asked.

"Other than Regan's dick?"

Now I *could* laugh. "Yeah, other than coming up with words for a guy's dick."

Ann shook her head, her brownish-red ringlets moving in one big curly mass. "Nothing. Absolutely nothing. Which is why we should go do something."

While my mom didn't much care, Ann's mom got all crabby when Ann didn't bring home any money because it meant she had to go out to get some spending cash herself instead of staying home polishing her jewelry.

"Like what?"

"Kmart. There's that one right on Broadway. Remember last year? It's always crowded—it's a cakewalk." Ann closed her notebook. "Come on. I need to get some new underwear if I'm ever gonna get your brother."

It was no secret to anybody—even to Jimmy—that Ann totally loved him. All you had to do was read a page from Ann's notebook to see that Regan was a dead ringer for Jimmy—the man who never wanted to settle down until he met Cynthia, aka Ann, the one woman who could change him. Ann wanted more than anything to be engaged to Jimmy, like I was to Patrick, especially since she was a few months older than me and Jimmy was a few months older than Patrick. But age didn't matter so much as the right match, and no one was anywhere near convinced Ann and Jimmy were right for each other, least of all Jimmy. But if Jimmy came around to it, my parents and the Murphys would think it was great because siblings marrying into the same families meant an even swap.

"All right," I said. "Let's go."

Ann stood up. "Cool. I'll get the baby carriage."

The carriage was the kind where you could close the top to keep your baby out of the sun or cold, and we kept it closed so that it seemed like the baby was sleeping. No one ever asked to see the baby because both of us looked too young to be mothers. They figured some loser boyfriend had knocked one of us up and then split, leaving us to drop out of school and raise the baby on welfare. Instead of asking if it was a boy or a girl or what the baby's name was, people shot us looks full of pity or sometimes even disgust and moved on fast.

Ann was right: the aisles teemed with tired women lugging screaming kids on their hips and old ladies shuffling on walkers. What few overwhelmed and underpaid workers there were couldn't care less about what we were doing.

Ann wheeled the carriage straight to the lingerie department. I looked around halfheartedly while Ann plucked pair after pair of panties and bras off the racks. I'd chosen only one plain white set when Ann dragged me into the dressing room, her arms full.

"Come on, Bridget." She handed me a black number with so much lace it might as well have been see-through. "Live a little."

I tried it on over my Jockeys and plain white bra as Ann modeled another black pair with a matching push-up bra. She twirled in front of the mirror, hands on her hips. "What do you think? Would Jimmy like this? Or maybe this?" She held up a thong.

Ann was really pretty and she didn't know it either, which made her even prettier. But Ann's looks didn't seem to matter to Jimmy. Of course I couldn't tell her that, so I just rolled my eyes and said, "Ann, he's my brother."

"So? Patrick's mine, and I know he'd like what you're wearing."

I started to wriggle out of the underwear. No way did I need to hear Ann talk about the power of Patrick's manliness.

"You better be taking those off to try more on."

When I gave her a look that said I was done, she whispered, "Bridge, you have to at least keep that pair. Come on!" So I shimmied back into the underwear and then pulled my shorts and shirt on. Ann pulled on one more pair over the first before putting her jean shorts and shirt back on.

As we walked out, Ann leaned close. "Okay, now it's time for some real shopping."

Since we'd just be returning them for cash, the trick was to take stuff that was hard to steal, like a tennis racket or a cooking pan. That way you got around needing a receipt. Most Country thieves just stuck to clothes. This time Ann went for a set of eight fancy glasses called double old-fashioneds. They were in a box, so it was easy to just slip the box inside the carriage when no one was looking, put the blanket over the box, and close the carriage again. One time we'd stolen a stereo with the baby carriage, but that wasn't something you could return—Jimmy sold that off in the parking lot of some beach we stopped at. I nabbed two silver-plated picture frames and a heinous bowl with strawberries painted on it. It was amazing what people paid good money for.

We picked up a pack of diapers and a little stuffed lion so we'd look legit. We paid in cash for the diapers and lion and headed to the parking lot. In the truck Ann totaled our loot. Sixty-nine dollars for the glasses, twenty-nine for the bowl, and nineteen per picture frame. Not bad for a morning's work.

Ann drove us back to the campground in her father's truck since she had an old license from one of her cousins. I drove sometimes too, but I didn't have a license. When we turned onto the road the campground was on, Ann kept going past the first entrance. I immediately knew why—Jimmy—and shot her a look.

"Let's just see if he's there."

"He's probably still asleep," I told Ann. "He was out again last night."

"So was Patrick," she said.

I waited, but Ann didn't say anything else. "Doesn't that make you mad?" I asked. It made me want to wreck something.

"Why?"

"You know what they do."

"It doesn't matter what they do now, Bridge. It matters who they marry."

It was nice if that made Ann feel better, but it did nothing for me. I didn't see why it was perfectly fine for Patrick to screw anyone he wanted—even Country girls—but I was supposed to stay as pure as pure could be until my wedding day. I wasn't even supposed to be with Patrick. How was that fair?

Ann stuck her head out the window as we rounded the bend to the trailer. "Jimmy!" she yelled. "We're coming to wake your ass up!"

Only as we turned the corner, we both saw that the trailer was missing, and so was Jimmy's truck. Ann braked, and we gaped at the empty spot where the trailer and truck had been.

"Holy shit," I gasped. "Dad is gonna freak."

"Maybe your mom took the trailer to show somebody."

"Mom just showed it this morning."

"Maybe they came back and bought it."

I shook my head, still staring at the empty spot. "He took it."

It was possible that the couple had come back and bought the trailer. And maybe Jimmy had gotten up early to go somewhere. But Mom only took cash, and Jimmy never woke before noon if he didn't have to. And anyway, I just knew. Jimmy was gone, and he'd taken Mom and Dad's trailer with him.

chapter 3

When Mom and Dad figured out that the trailer was missing and so was Jimmy, Dad smashed a lamp and kicked the front of the stove. Usually when Jimmy left it was only for a day or so, but three days later he still wasn't back. Dad called some of our cousins who lived in Murphy Village, the biggest Traveler settlement in the South, to ask if they'd seen or heard from him. He even tracked down Big Jim, which was saying a lot because Dad would rather roll buck naked in a hill of fire ants than talk to Big Jim. Big Jim said he hadn't seen Jimmy or heard from him either.

Dad said he'd about done all the roofing he could and it was time to move on. He said we were going to leave without Jimmy, which was just plain fine with me. In fact, I hoped we *did*. As far as I was concerned, Jimmy deserved to have us leave his ass behind.

"He's gotta be coming back, Douglas," Mom pleaded. "He wouldn't just up and take the trailer without a plan."

"So he gets back and we're gone. It'd serve him right," Dad snapped.

"He's only eighteen," Mom argued.

"When I was eighteen, I was on my own."

"That was different."

"Yeah, I didn't go around stealing my father's trailers," Dad said with a sneer. "If he's gonna run off, then let him see if he can be the man he's so sure he is."

Mom sighed. "Let's give him a few more days."

This just about killed me. Only Jimmy could run off with the trailer Mom had practically sold and still have her plugging for him.

"Fine, but when he gets back, he better have a damn good story to tell, and he better start showing some goddamn respect around here," Dad grumbled.

And Dad! I couldn't believe he caved too. I guess it was because he knew Mom loved Jimmy more than anything, no matter what kind of shit Jimmy gave her. But the whole thing just made me crazy because I knew it would be completely different if I'd run off with their trailer.

Since we could be leaving any day, Ann and I decided to return the stuff to Kmart. Just in case anyone remembered us, we waited until the late afternoon so it was a different shift and the same people weren't working. The store also wouldn't be as crowded around dinnertime, and we needed the cashier to take the time to hear our story.

Mr. Murphy was still out with the truck, so we needed a ride or else we'd be hitching, and that was never a good idea in case someone caught on and you needed to bolt. Mom said Patrick was washing Dad's truck near the campground office, and we figured we'd go ask him for a lift. Patrick washed the truck almost every day that he and Dad used it because it was important to have it looking good for the jobs. As my fiancé, Patrick worked with my dad instead of his own dad. Our engagement was like a trial period for Dad to see if Patrick was a good worker—if he brought in enough money. If he did, we'd be married, and then Patrick would be part of our family. He'd work with my dad and eventually take over for him. That's the way it worked, with the groom going into the bride's family. Some parents even offered a dowry, or what was called a bride-price, to the parents who were giving up their son, but that was kind of old-fashioned, and I didn't think Dad had offered the Murphys one.

On the walk over to the office, we passed all the other campers. It was still early in the season, so the campground wasn't bumper-to-bumper trailers, but people were drifting in. There were gray-haired couples in shiny sweat suits, like the ones who wanted to buy Mom's trailer, touring the country while they could still move around okay. There were washed-out women with screaming husbands and babies dressed in diapers and nothing else on their way somewhere new to see if life would be better for them. And there were other Travelers. If they were Northern Travelers, chances were pretty good we knew them. If they were from another part of the country or if they were Scottish instead of Irish, we wouldn't know them, but we'd still be able to tell they were Travelers by the way they kept the spot around their trailers neat and clean, usually with a little Madonna statue out front and center. We could also tell by the way they talked and the way they kept to themselves and kept away from Country folk.

We passed Peggy Carroll, who was just a few years younger than us, hanging clothes on a line outside a trailer.

"How long have the Carrolls been here?" I asked Ann as Peggy waved to us, her ponytail bobbing.

"Yesterday," Ann said. "My dad already told 'em they might as well move on because we've already done all there is can be done here. They're leaving tomorrow for Mississippi."

Patrick had his shirt off and was soaping down the truck. His chest was still pale from the winter, not yet tanned from a summer under the harsh Southern sun. But his stomach and arms were toned from working day after day swabbing sealant on driveways and roofs, and I felt like running to him and kissing him, just because I could. *Soon I'd lie next to him every night,* I thought. Right then that didn't seem too rough, and I couldn't believe that out of all the Traveler girls, a lot of them prettier than me, I was going to be Patrick's wife. Of course, it'd been a match, but Patrick had to want it.

"We need a ride," Ann called to him.

Patrick stopped spraying and turned to us. He pointed the nozzle of the hose at me like it was a gun. "Give me all your money and all your gum."

I laughed. Patrick could be like that sometimes—totally goofy. I liked that about him more than anything. Definitely more than the things I was supposed to like about him, like that he was a hard worker and respected Traveler life. "Don't spray me!" I squealed.

Patrick lowered the hose and dried his hands on his gray cargo work pants with the big pockets and the loops on the sides. "Where you going?"

Ann held up the bag from Kmart. We had a big supply of Kmart bags and Wal-Mart bags too so we could use them to re-turn stuff.

Patrick said he'd drive us, and we waited while he finished up. Ann let me get in the truck first, so I sat in the middle next to Patrick. He'd put his shirt back on, but I could still smell the salt of his sweat.

"Where do you think Jimmy is?" Ann asked as we pulled out of the campground. I wasn't sure if she was talking to Patrick or me, so I kept quiet. I also didn't particularly care. I only cared when he'd get his ass back so Mom and Dad would chill out. Patrick didn't answer either, and Ann reached behind me and poked his shoulder.

"I don't know," he said. "Probably in Alabama or Tennessee, pulling some shit off. Maybe he met up with some others."

Ann leaned back in her seat. "I hope he's careful."

"Jimmy?" I snorted. "Unlikely. Crazy, stupid, yes. But careful? Not Jimmy."

Ann shook her head. "You're starting to sound just like your dad."

"Well, maybe he's right when it comes to Jimmy." I almost started to tell Ann about the other night at dinner and how Dad said if Jimmy didn't settle down he'd make a match for him. I was going to tell her that she should want him to be crazy so Dad would match them up. But I decided it was better if Ann didn't know.

When we got to Kmart, Patrick stayed in the car. This time it was important that we weren't with a guy. It was also important we didn't have the baby carriage.

The second we walked in the store, we searched the cashiers' faces. I started at the end closest to us: older woman with hair helmet—no way. Middle-aged man with ugly checkered vest—not great. Ann must've started from the farthest aisle because she whispered, "Got him. Aisle seven."

I looked at aisle 7. Ann was right. He was perfect. Maybe sixteen, skinny, bad bowl haircut that his mama probably gave him, and braces.

Ann fluffed her hair, arched her back so her boobs were the first thing Bowl Boy would see, and headed off to aisle 7. I followed her, and when we got to the register, I hoisted the bag onto the counter.

"Hi," Ann cooed sweetly. "We need to make a return."

Bowl Boy reached into the bag and pulled out the double old-fashioneds, the frames, and the bowl. "Well, okay, do you have a receipt?"

"It was a gift," Ann said. "From my aunt. I don't know what she was thinking—that I'd want this old-lady stuff, you know?"

Bowl Boy nodded. "Totally. Did you want to look around for something else? Or I can give you store credit?"

Ann looked to me and then back to Bowl Boy. She leaned toward him like she was confiding in him, sharing something she wouldn't share with just anybody. "My friend and I, we kind of need the money, you know?"

"Well, it's just I'm not supposed to—" Bowl Boy started saying.

Ann cut him off. "Listen, is there any way? I mean, my friend here, she's kind of in a *bind,* if you know what I mean. And her boyfriend, he just said, 'Take care of it yourself.' And we're gonna take care of it, but we need money to do that. And then my aunt gives me these things for my birthday that I don't want at all."

Bowl Boy nodded along. Ann had him going all right.

"I mean, what good are old-lady cups? Do you think there's anything you can do to help us out?"

Bowl Boy inhaled, held it, and sighed. He looked around,

27

then turned back to the register and punched in some special code, and the cash drawer popped open. "No problem," he said. I could tell from his expression he thought he was being all superhero-like. That he was doing his part to make up for the shithead guys who always get the girls even though he'd treat a girl a hundred times better and never get her pregnant. He handed us the cash and said, more to me this time than to Ann, "Good luck, you know, with *everything*."

"Thanks," I said.

We waited to laugh until we got into the truck. "Oh my God," Ann giggled. "That was too easy."

"It was sort of sad. Did you see the way he looked at me? He thought he was saving the day."

"You two breaking some young guy's heart again?" Patrick asked.

"Nah," Ann said. "He'll live. Plus he'll be talking about this to all his friends for weeks."

Patrick looped his arm around me. "Just don't go breaking this guy's heart."

He took his hand back to start the truck, and he didn't look like he was joking anymore. He looked like he was actually worried I might break his heart, which made *my* heart soften. Every time I freaked at the *M* word, I'd see him looking so good or he'd do something so funny or sweet, and then it felt like he was slowly winning my heart, piece by tiny piece.

Suddenly I didn't want to lose that feeling of falling for Patrick. I wanted to do something normal, something everyday. Something besides scamming Kmarts or paving driveways. Something a Country girl would do with her Country boyfriend. "Let's not go back just yet."

"But what about Jimmy?" Ann said.

"What about him?" Like I owed Jimmy a damn thing.

"What if he's back?"

"Then he'll still be there when we get back."

"Where we going?" Patrick asked, all eager.

I turned to Ann. "Remember that swimming hole?"

She nodded but gave me a look to make sure I wouldn't spill about the cute Country boys we'd met there on a real hot day last summer. They were about our age and were smoking dope and fishing for bass. We lied about who we were and flirted a little, and it was fun to pretend to be someone else for a while. Nothing happened—we just talked with them. We wouldn't have let anything happen. But just talking to Country folk, especially Country boys, was forbidden, unless you had to for some reason.

"Where is it?" Patrick asked.

Ann told him where to go, and as we headed out of the parking lot, Patrick said, "You still reading that book? The one about the Black Sox?"

I nodded. Usually Patrick didn't really care about the books I read or books in general, but he liked hearing about this one because it was about baseball. Most Travelers were into football, especially the Fighting Irish, but with Patrick it was always baseball. He didn't have a favorite team and he hadn't really ever played ball as far as I could remember, except maybe for campground games of smacking rocks or soda cans with sticks. But he watched games on TV and collected cards. Other people probably thought he collected them to forge the autographs and then resell them, but I knew he was just keeping them for himself. It seemed like he should've grown out of collecting them or grown out of being able to come up with this or that player's batting average or RBIs from a given year, or maybe it seemed strange that he even cared. But it was the one thing he did seem to care about—besides maybe me—and I was glad he at least had that one thing.

"They really throw the Series?" Patrick asked.

"Who cares!" Ann blurted.

"I do. And Bridget does . . . right?"

I nodded. "I guess some of them did, but others just said they were going to and then they played really well. Like Joe Jackson. He hit .375 with twelve hits and six RBIs."

Patrick shook his head. "Still. How could you do that? I mean, throw the World Series?"

We parked alongside the road because it wasn't an official swimming hole but just a spot through the woods with a few rocks you could dive off and a little sand that was more like gravel. We walked out to the rocks, and I started taking off my shoes and socks.

"You're going in?" Patrick asked.

It wasn't that hot out—the summer heat and humidity hadn't set in yet—but I loved the water, and any chance I got to swim, I took.

When I stood up and started to pull my shirt over my head, Ann whooped. "You taking it all off?" She glanced at Patrick. "I know someone who'd like that."

I rolled my eyes. "No." I was wearing a sports bra underneath my T-shirt, and I left my shorts on. The one good thing about being tall was my stomach—it was flat and long, and I actually kind of liked it. I walked out to the edge of the water and was about to dive off when Patrick yelled, "Wait!"

I turned back to him. "What?"

"You sure that's safe? You don't know how deep it is—what if there're rocks down there?"

We'd dove off the same rocks last year, and I couldn't believe that much had changed. Plus, wasn't that the whole point? Chancing it? I shrugged, turned from Patrick, and dove in. The water was cool and delicious, like Italian ice on a sweltering day. Instead of coming up, I stayed under as long as I could, until my lungs were about to explode. I imagined Patrick up there worrying about me, waiting for me to come up. There was something about the way he was always so careful and cautious that made me want to press him.

When I couldn't stand it anymore, I surfaced—just in time to see Patrick jump in feetfirst, sending a wave of water against the rocks. He'd kicked off his shoes but still had his shirt and pants on.

"What the fuck were you doing?" Patrick demanded when he came out of the water and saw that I was fine.

"Just messing around. Relax."

Patrick swam toward me.

"So you *can* swim," I teased. "I thought maybe you didn't want me to go in because you couldn't."

"Of course I can," he said. "I thought you'd hit your head and I was gonna have to save your ass."

"Save me, save me!" I mocked, laughing.

Patrick dove down and grabbed my legs. I let him pull me under, opened my eyes in the murky water, and looked at him.

When we'd both come up again, Ann called to us from the rocks. "It's spooky up here without you guys."

"Well, then come in," I yelled back.

"It's too cold," she called. "Come on back."

"We better get back anyway," Patrick said. "Your father's gonna wonder where the truck is."

"He doesn't need it now." Dad was no doubt already a few

beers into his nightly routine. What was there to go back for? To watch?

"Still, we should go just in case."

I splashed him. "Always the responsible one."

He splashed me back. "Well, someone has to be, don't they?"

"Guess so," I said, and started breaststroking back to the rocks. But I wasn't so sure. Most people would have said that everything we did was risky, but I was beginning to feel that it was just the opposite—that everything we did felt too safe. Too predictable.

Patrick busted into a fast crawl, peeling through the water, and reached the rocks before me. He got out first and held out his hand to me. With his hair slicked back, his eyes looked even more amazing than they usually did. Even though I didn't need his help, I let him pull me up. It was obvious I'd scared him, and I figured I'd let him feel like the big man for once.

We tried to wring out our clothes, but we still soaked the bench of the truck driving back. At the campground Ann went home, leaving Patrick and me to dry off the seats together.

"See, isn't this summer already turning out to be fun?" he asked.

"I guess so," I said.

But swimming didn't feel like enough. Something was still missing. Patrick and Ann obviously didn't feel it. Maybe I was crazy. All things considered, the summer really *wasn't* starting out too bad, except of course for Jimmy stealing the trailer and going God knows where. But there was something more. Something just out of reach that I wanted to touch.

chapter 4

A few more days of waiting around for Jimmy and we were all going crazy. If Jimmy had been home, I'd have killed him myself and saved Dad the trouble.

The couple who looked at the trailer called back wanting to buy it, but Mom had to tell them we'd already sold it. Dad and Patrick stopped looking for jobs because there weren't any left. Mom and Dad stomped around the trailer, letting the screen door slam on their way in or out. They talked in short, abrupt jabs—to each other and to me when I was around, which wasn't often because I tried to always be somewhere else.

Ann, Patrick, and I were sitting outside the Murphys' trailer playing poker when Patrick decided we should do a pigeon drop.

"I'm sick of doing nothing," he said. "We can at least pull in a little cash."

Welcome to our life, I wanted to tell him. *Bor-ing.* When we weren't in school, there was nothing to do but work stores, and most days we just sat around and killed time.

"A pigeon drop?" I said skeptically. The only pigeon drop

we'd ever pulled had been with Jimmy, and as much as I hated to admit it, I wasn't sure we could do one without him.

"We can do it. We don't need Jimmy," Patrick said, reading my mind.

"Think of what he'll say when he gets back—he won't believe we pulled it off without him," Ann gushed at the prospect of surprising and impressing Jimmy.

I didn't know why I gave in because the whole way out to the Wal-Mart all I was thinking was how if we screwed up and got caught or had to ditch town, Mom and Dad would kill me. They were already on edge because of Jimmy, and I was supposed to stick to small jobs like ripping off stores where if you got caught you cried and begged and told some story about your father gambling away all the rent money and they usually let you off. But by the time we rolled into the lot at the Wal-Mart I'd figured out why I'd agreed even though I wasn't sure we could do it alone. I'd agreed because screw them. Jimmy wasn't the only one who could do something he wasn't supposed to.

We searched for our pigeon half the day because choosing the right person was the most important part. Scams didn't work because they were that good, necessarily. They worked because the person you scammed was pathetic and wanted to believe that what you promised was real.

We parked in the shade because it was a sweltering day, a sign that summer was here to stay. But by late morning, the shade was long gone, and even with the windows rolled down my sweaty thighs stuck to the truck seat. I was supposed to be looking for the pigeon, but I'd pretty much given up. Ann was scribbling in her notebook, stopping to read us parts every now and then.

"This is good, isn't it? 'Cynthia was striking in a way that only someone with bountiful breasts could be.' "

I laughed and then covered my mouth with my hand.

"What are you laughing at?"

" 'Bountiful breasts'?" Ann had definitely given herself an upgrade.

Before Ann could get mad, Patrick craned his head out the window and announced, "There she is."

He was looking at an old geezer who'd pulled into the lot in a blue LeSabre with a dented front fender. We were behind her and we watched as she parked, cut the engine, and pulled out one of those minimagazines filled with romance stories that you pick up at a supermarket checkout, like the kind Ann tried to write. Patrick smiled. "A perfect pigeon."

We waited another twenty minutes, watching. We had to give it some time before we went to work on her. Otherwise she'd think it was strange that we'd approached her the minute she'd driven in. And we also had to make sure we'd picked the right pigeon. She didn't get out of the car but took out a neatly wrapped sandwich, probably tuna fish, and just sat there reading the minimag and munching away. She was at least seventy, judging from her wiry orange hair and hunched shoulders. She did seem like a perfect pigeon—didn't have anything to do in the middle of the week but sit around in the parking lot of the Wal-Mart waiting for something to happen. And her bad dye job and dented car showed she could use the money. We couldn't be sure she'd go for it, but she looked worth a try.

We drove the truck to the other side of the parking lot, out of the pigeon's sight.

"How's it gonna work?" Ann asked.

"Bridget'll go," Patrick said. "Then I'll follow up. You stay in the truck."

"Why not me and Bridget, or me and you?"

"Me and you look too much alike, and you and Bridget, no way. It makes it seem more likely if there's a guy."

"Fine," Ann muttered, pulling her notebook back out and getting a stick of gum from her purse.

I got out of the truck, taking the envelope of cash we'd prepared—three *kade* in total. Twenty-six hundred Patrick had earned working driveways this past winter, my two hundred from Mrs. C. and the store, and the hundred seventeen Ann and I'd made at Kmart.

I took a deep breath and thought how Ann wouldn't have the knot in her stomach that I had in mine. *Get tough*, I told myself. *Be smooth.*

I acted like I was just walking by the pigeon's car, looking more interested in the envelope than anything else. But then I stopped, like I was noticing the woman for the first time. And I *was* noticing her for the first time up close. She wasn't fragile, just old; not so much like someone's granny but more tough and weathered. This was good because if she was tough she probably wouldn't get scared and might go for it.

I stared down at the envelope, turning it over in my hands, pretending I'd just found it.

"I can't believe this," I mumbled, sort of to myself but loud enough for her to hear. Then I turned to her with my best look of surprise. "I can't believe this. I just found an awful lot of money."

I opened the envelope and she peeked in at the bills. At the sight of all that green, she straightened up and slipped her minimag onto the passenger seat. "Oh, my."

36

Bam! She was interested.

As I delivered my next line, Patrick walked up from behind us right on cue. "I found it on the ground over there, right behind that truck." I pointed to a Ford a few spots back. "It was just lying there—all this money."

Patrick pretended he was walking by but then stopped at the mention of money. "You found some money?"

I looked at him a little skeptically and then said, "Yeah."

"Let me see."

I showed him the envelope.

"Holy shit. That's gotta be close to three grand. What're you gonna do?"

I shrugged and looked at the entrance to Wal-Mart. "I guess I'll take it inside and see if anybody lost it."

"Don't be stupid," Patrick said. "You found it."

Right then was key. We'd see whether the pigeon would bite. If she didn't, we'd just picked the wrong person, that's all. We'd go back to the truck and wait for a new pigeon. It wasn't about only one shot. It was trial and error. With Jimmy it'd taken four tries before we found a pigeon who went for it. I held my breath, hoping. Bite, bite, bite.

The pigeon shrugged. "Finders keepers, right?"

Yes! Now we were rolling, and all my nerves disappeared. I motioned to the Wal-Mart. "I don't know. I work there. I think I'll just go see if anybody lost an envelope full of money. I won't say how much or anything. If no one lost it, then I guess I'll keep it." Here I laughed nervously. "Maybe I'll even share it with you guys."

I was playing innocent and I was nailing it. I jogged inside, leaving Patrick to do his thing. He would say to the pigeon, *"I could use some money right now. How 'bout you?"* Hopefully she'd

37

agree. Maybe she was thinking about finally fixing the dent in her car or about dyeing her hair right.

After a few minutes inside Wal-Mart looking at greeting cards, I came back out with the envelope tucked deep into the pocket of my shorts. Patrick looked disappointed, but that was just part of the act. The best part was that the pigeon's face fell too. Excitement rushed through me. That familiar buzz when you know you're this close to pulling it off. When you know you've got somebody who'll do whatever you want.

"Look," I explained, "I left it inside at my station. Nobody's lost an envelope, but it's too risky, just taking it, don't you think? What if the real owner shows up? What if the owner goes to the cops and they ask around?"

"Are you kidding?" Patrick moaned. "Who leaves three grand lying around in a parking lot? It's obviously drug money or something like that. No one's gonna claim it."

Patrick was on his game and we were clicking.

"I don't know," I said. "It still seems risky."

Patrick nodded. "Okay, look, I've got fifteen hundred of my own money with me—my brother just paid me back on a loan. I was headed in to buy new tires, but I'll tell you what. I'll add my money to the money you found, and we'll split it down the middle. Then you and I agree that we won't spend it for a week, and then if in a week we don't hear anything about it being anyone else's, it's ours. This way you don't go it alone. If the cops start looking around, then I'll be in on it too."

"Like then you'd be sharing the risk?" I asked, still hesitant.

"Exactly."

I paused, pretending to think it over, before saying, "Okay."

Patrick pulled out his wallet and started fingering the bills.

He nodded for me to walk away with him. "Come on, let's get out of this nice woman's way."

"Wait a second." I looked from Patrick to the pigeon. "She was here before you—what about her?"

"But she's not willing to put up her own money as good faith. *I am.*"

"Well, maybe she is." I turned back to the pigeon. "Are you?"

"I guess, yeah," the pigeon said. She was sinking deeper into the scam. "But I don't have that kind of cash on me."

We were almost there. "Well, could you get some?" I asked. "There's got to be an ATM around here, right?"

It was no coincidence that there was an ATM right next to the Wal-Mart. Patrick pointed to it. "There's one right over there."

"Okay," the pigeon said, scrambling from her car. "It'll just take me a second." Standing next to us, she was shorter, smaller somehow. Her legs were little toothpicks and she teetered as she scurried over to the ATM.

When she came back a few minutes later, she showed us her money.

Patrick cautioned, "Don't go waving it around like that. Here, I'll put it with my money."

He took the bills and put them in the envelope along with his money and stuffed the envelope in the back pocket of his work pants. It was done—we had the money. Now we just had to get rid of the pigeon.

"Wait a second," I said warily. "I think I'd feel better if you didn't keep all the money. Give her the money."

Patrick reached into his pocket again, but it was his left pocket this time, not his right. The pigeon didn't notice. He pulled out an identical envelope stuffed with blank paper and handed it to her. "Put it in your purse or something, though. Before anyone sees it."

The pigeon dropped the envelope in her purse.

Patrick rubbed his hands together. "Now let's go inside and get the rest of our money."

It was my turn, my line. But suddenly, looking at the pigeon—her orange hair with the gray roots showing through—I hesitated. Could we, could I, do this to her?

But it was too late. We'd already done it.

Patrick cleared his throat and eyed me. "Let's go."

"Wait," I said, finally coming through with my line. "I have to get something from my car."

Patrick motioned to the pigeon. "You go ahead in, I'll wait here for her, and then we'll come in and we'll all get the money."

Since she believed she held both her money and Patrick's, the pigeon thought nothing of it and walked off toward the entrance to the Wal-Mart. I headed to the truck, where Ann sat ready in the driver's seat. Patrick waited a few seconds for the pigeon to go inside and then ran to the truck too. He jumped in next to me, Ann started the engine, and we took off. At first there was only that buzz again—of not getting caught and, for me at least, of doing something you weren't sure you could do, something you weren't supposed to do. Pure adrenaline. Running, floating, flying.

We couldn't just go back to the campground—that wouldn't have felt like celebrating—so we hit the highway and just drove. Ann pumped the gas and the speedometer crept up to over eighty, which was pretty unbelievable for an old piece-of-shit Dodge truck. The whole thing rattled but we didn't care. Patrick took out the money and counted it—we'd made fifteen hundred dollars. Most people scored double or triple that on pigeon drops, but for us, it was about just doing it more than the amount of the take.

Patrick whistled. "Not bad."

"She's probably still there waiting," Ann laughed. "Pathetic."

"Or she took the envelope out and saw that it's just paper," Patrick said.

Ann shook her head. "That's the only thing. I wish we could see them after too."

Patrick leaned over and kissed me, first on the cheek and then on the lips. We kissed heavier and Patrick snaked his hand up my back, drawing me to him. The floating feeling of what we'd just done became floating away with Patrick. That is, until Ann yelled, "Enough already! Get a room!"

Patrick pulled away and we tore down the highway feeling like nothing could ever slow us down. Ann tuned the radio to country western and we blared it and just drove. Usually I couldn't stand country—that and classic rock were pretty much the only music played in the South. In Miami, we got all kinds of stations—Top 40, hip-hop, alternative. I didn't so much like one type but liked being able to switch around. But it was still early in the summer and I wasn't totally sick of twangy songs about love gone wrong yet. Plus, not even a bad song could squelch the feeling I had right then. Maybe this was what I'd been missing— maybe this was why Jimmy was sick of doing driveways.

We finally got back to the campground around six o'clock. By that time I was crashing from my high. I walked back from Patrick and Ann's trailer with my share of the money, but I didn't even care about the cash anymore. I couldn't get the pigeon out of my head—her toothpick legs and orange hair. Thoughts seeped in, thoughts I wasn't supposed to be having. Like what if she really needed the money? Maybe she needed an operation and couldn't afford it and that's why she was sitting at Wal-Mart just doing nothing because there was nothing she *could* do. Maybe she'd thought we were God or fate sending her a miracle. I wanted to laugh the way Ann did, but instead the floating feeling turned to a dull ache in my chest.

She was probably fine. *Just wanted the cash,* I told myself. She probably had plenty of money but was one of those people who never spent a dime and always wanted more. We needed the money just as much as she did.

The pain in my chest eased as I reached the trailer door. Through the screen I heard Mom and Dad talking about Jimmy.

"So what're you gonna do?" Mom said.

Maybe he was back or Dad had heard from him.

"First thing tomorrow I'm talking to the Murphys. Next spring would be fine for a wedding."

Shit! Ann would be so happy she wouldn't know what to do with herself. But Jimmy—I didn't want to be around when Dad broke the news to him.

"Spring?" Mom gasped. "She's awfully young."

"You were *thirteen.*"

Mom continued, "But like I said with Jimmy, things are different now. It's not the way it used to be. I just don't know if Bridget's ready. . . ."

I froze. The pain in my chest surged back. I let go of the door handle and sank down on the trailer steps.

The date was supposed to be set at the *end* of the summer. Not the beginning. And spring was only a year away. Why did Dad want to push things along so badly? That wouldn't give me time to figure everything out. And I still needed time. One minute I was falling in love with Patrick and wanted to be his wife; the next I wasn't sure I could be anybody's wife. Was it just about not having a choice? Was it Patrick? Or was it me?

chapter 5

Ann was the one who told me. It'd been a week since the pigeon drop. A week since I'd overheard Mom and Dad, and still not a word to me on the date being set. I'd killed time mostly by reading, but I'd just finished *Eight Men Out* and *The Autobiography of Malcolm X,* another book I'd taken out of the school library and obviously wouldn't be returning anytime soon. Since it wasn't sweltering yet, I was on a towel in my bikini trying to wipe out my farmer's tan. It was nice, just lying there with the sun warming my skin, breathing in the tangy smell of Coppertone. I had my CD player next to me and I was listening to an old Sinéad O'Connor CD that I'd bought at this really cool used-CD store all the Country kids at school went to. I closed my eyes and pretended I was at the beach with the rolling ocean only a few feet in front of me, instead of on the scorched crabgrass next to a tin trailer.

Ann bounced up in her cutoff shorts and a multicolored striped tank top. She looked even more beautiful than usual because her smile was taking over her whole face.

"Guess who's back?" she whispered so Mom and Dad inside the trailer wouldn't hear.

"Really?"

Ann nodded. I threw on my T-shirt and shorts, which stuck to my Coppertoned skin, and followed Ann to the other side of the campground. On our way through the dusty grounds littered with cigarette butts and soda cans we passed a Traveler couple. I couldn't remember their first names, but I was pretty sure they were Sherlocks. Maybe Mikey Boy's clan. They were screaming at each other in front of their trailer. It wasn't even noon and the man had a bottle of cheap, no-name whiskey in his hand.

"If you'd keep your mouth shut!" he yelled.

"And if you'd *do* something for a change!" she cried back at him.

Regular lovebirds. Ann and I walked faster, our eyes glued to our feet. When we'd passed them, I said, "I can't wait to get out of this place." But it wasn't the place. As if it was that easy. Leaving seemed like the greatest thing right then. But the next stop down the road wouldn't look that different. Or the place after that. It never did. There'd always be couples like that, and someday I might be half of one.

Jimmy was slouched in his truck, a straw hat tipped over his face, shielding his eyes from the sun. He needed a shave. His stubble was darker than his hair, which was the color of a dirt road in mud season, but he still looked good. My brother could be a jerk sometimes—and a selfish jerk at that—but he had a way about him. A glint of trouble in his eyes, but the kind of trouble that drew girls in.

Ann leaned her forearms on the driver's-side window frame and stared at him. He could probably feel her breath, but he

44

didn't move. Without lifting the hat or turning his head—I'm not sure how he even knew I was there—Jimmy spoke to me: "Are they *narked*, Bridget?"

Narked was Cant for pissed off good. Jimmy didn't know much Cant. None of us did, really, just a few words. Mostly it was the older generations who spoke it, especially when they didn't want Country folk to understand. But Jimmy always showed off by using what little he knew.

"You could say that," I laughed.

This was enough to make Jimmy sit up and flip off the hat. "Well, they won't be pissed when they see this." He reached under the seat and ka-thumped a stack of bills at least three inches thick onto the dashboard.

"Holy shit!" Ann squealed, her eyes widening. "How did you get all that?"

She reached into the truck for the money but Jimmy playfully slapped her wrist. Ann pulled back her hand and Jimmy settled into his seat.

"Well, if you really want to know, first I sold Mom's trailer—for much more than she was asking. Then I picked up another trailer and sold that."

"From a manufacturer?" Ann asked.

It was a stupid question that Jimmy didn't bother answering. He meant lifted. Trailers were pretty easy to take. If people didn't lock them, you just backed your truck up to them and hooked right up. And if they were locked, a crowbar did the trick just fine.

"Sold that one," Jimmy continued. "Then I came up with the best score ever. I was driving past this tree farm and I saw all the fields with the little baby trees in them. And it didn't really hit me till later when I was checking out the neighborhoods and I got on this road full of huge rich-people houses. I mean real rich people. Three- and four-car garages, that kind of shit. And they had all this landscaping, trees and bushes and flowers. But there were some houses that had better landscaping than others, and that's when it hit me. That night I went back to the tree place, found a bunch of buckets, and cut down about thirty trees. It wasn't that hard 'cause they were saplings and all. Put them each in a bucket with some dirt, and the next day I went back to that road to one of the houses that looked like it wasn't as done up as the others. Sold that guy ten trees, another guy ten, and a woman ten. Plopped them in and that was that." Jimmy cackled. "You know, the woman was the funniest. I was explaining to her about watering the trees real good for the first ten days or else they wouldn't grow. And she gets out a pad to take notes! Country folk—you gotta love 'em. And the rich ones are even stupider. I'd love to see what happens when all those trees die. I bet she goes back to her notes to see what she did wrong. She probably still hasn't figured out they don't have roots!"

"Well," Ann said after Jimmy had finished. "Aren't you going to ask us what we did while you were gone?"

"Let me guess," Jimmy said with a sneer. "Sat around and ripped off the Kmart?"

Before Ann could blab about the pigeon drop—which, compared to Jimmy's take, suddenly didn't seem like much—I blurted out, "You gonna come tell Mom and Dad you're back?"

"They around?"

I nodded.

"Dad too?"

"No more work left. . . . We've been here over a week . . . waiting for *you*."

Jimmy grabbed the cash and opened the truck door. "Well, I might as well make their day."

I followed Jimmy to the trailer. Dad was watching TV. Well, really he was snoring in front of the TV. Mom had her ledger and her calculator out and was going over the bills. Like most Traveler women, Mom tracked all our finances. Dad brought in most of the money, but Mom knew what we could spend it on. She also invested some of our money in stocks. Some Travelers didn't know about stuff like that or didn't trust banks, but smarter ones, like Mom, did.

When she saw Jimmy, Mom dropped her pen, leapt up, and hugged him. Jimmy held her face in his hands and kissed her on the cheek so that it made a big smacking sound. Then he plunked the money down on the counter. Mom snatched it up and started counting the bills. "There better be seventeen *kade* for my trailer."

Jimmy puffed out his chest. "There's way more than that."

Now awake, Dad got up. Seeing them standing eye to eye, I noticed Dad wasn't much taller than Jimmy anymore. And next to Jimmy Dad looked weary, like an old beat-up car with bald tires and peeling paint.

"You don't take off," Dad said, deadpan. "And you sure as hell don't take *my* property."

Mom held up the money she was counting. "But look at all this, Douglas."

"I would've called, but I knew you'd just tell me to get back," Jimmy added.

Dad glared at Jimmy. "Damn right I would have. We're a family, and you're supposed to be helping out around here."

Jimmy squinted. He clenched his hands in tight fists. I braced myself for what would come next.

"I don't help out?" He opened a fist and pointed to the bills Mom was still riffling through. "That's more *kush* than you've ever seen at one time."

"Where'd you get it?" Dad demanded.

"I worked for it. Same as always."

"Doing what? You don't make that kind of *kush* doing driveways."

"No, you don't."

Dad's tone grew fiercer. "You better not be selling."

Mom stopped counting the money, and her face turned white. "Oh, Jesus, Mary, and Joseph."

To Mom drugs meant one thing and one thing only: serious jail time. Even though the good money in drugs sometimes tempted Travelers, most knew to stay away from it.

"Why can't you believe this is legit?" Jimmy said. But he didn't leave room for Dad to answer. "You know why? Because you could never pull in this kind of money. Because you're jealous. You're small-time. And you can't handle it that I'm big-time. That I'm—"

Jimmy didn't get to finish. Dad lunged for him, his eyes wild. But he didn't get his hands around Jimmy's neck. Jimmy pulled back the hand that was still balled in a fist and slammed Dad across the bridge of his nose. There must've been a whole lot of power behind that punch, because it knocked Dad straight back onto the floor. A trickle of blood soon became a stream that ran from his nose. Dad touched his finger to it and brought his hand in front of his eyes, as if he had to see the red to be sure Jimmy had made him bleed.

Dad lay sprawled on the floor. Jimmy's eyes were wide. He was scared of what he'd just done. My heart pounded. I'd seen plenty of our people fight over the years. I even saw Dad and

Big Jim go at it once, Big Jim cracking three of Dad's ribs and blackening one eye. And even though it wasn't nearly as bad when they were sober as when they were drunk, our people were always rough when they fought, their instinct always to go for the kill. Dad had shoved Jimmy before, and Jimmy had thrown things or stormed out, but neither had ever thrown punches. I wasn't scared to be in the middle of it; I'd been there before. But this time Jimmy had crossed the line. I'd thought I'd wanted him to, but now, looking at Dad, I wasn't so sure.

Mom sat frozen. Jimmy gazed helplessly at her and then backed out of the trailer. The screen door slapped behind him. Mom stood and went to Dad. He shook her off. "It's nothing. Just a bleeder."

Mom handed him a dish towel and he pressed it against his nose. Blood seeped through it so that when Dad turned to me, the red in the towel was all I saw below his angry eyes.

"We're goddamn lucky you're marrying good," he said.

chapter 6

Your father's right, you know," Mom said after Dad took the wad of money he'd scoffed at and left. She was washing the bloody dish towel in the sink. She squeezed it under the spray of the faucet, the water running into the drain a dull rust color. "Thank God for Patrick. Jimmy's wild. I wish he weren't, but he's just like his uncle. We need someone who'll take care of things."

"What do you think's gonna happen?" I asked. "I mean with Jimmy and Dad." I still saw Dad's face clearly as he lunged at Jimmy and Jimmy's when he'd seen what he'd done. I wondered if things between them could ever be okay.

"I don't know."

"Is Dad gonna make him marry Ann?"

"I don't know if he can."

Mom paused, her eyes watery, and then she wrung out the dish towel.

"Mom? What was it like when you married Dad?"

I didn't necessarily want to ask her about marriage, but there was no one else to ask. Sometimes I thought about asking one of my cousins. They'd been through it all. But I hadn't seen any of them in a while, and soon it'd be too late.

"What do you mean?"

"Did you love him?"

"I didn't even know your father. Not like you know Patrick. I'd only met him a handful of times."

"So wasn't that weird? I mean, all of a sudden you were married."

Mom lowered the dish towel and turned from the sink to face me. "Patrick's a good boy, Bridget. And he'll make you a good husband. It's not always gonna be easy for you, but this is good for all of us, me and your father too. You're doing what's right for your people, which is exactly what I did. And life has worked out fine for me, hasn't it?"

I wondered why Mom had to ask me. Why she couldn't answer that question for herself. I hoped she'd say something else, like how she had come to love Dad so easily and how I would surely come to love Patrick.

But she didn't, and before I could decide whether to ask more, Mom's cell phone rang. She dried her hands and answered. "Hello? Hang on." Mom covered the receiver and said to me, "Business."

That was my cue to leave. When it came time to talk about money, Mom and Dad never wanted Jimmy and me around. We weren't even allowed to answer Mom's phone and had to ask special permission to use it. Usually when Mom said "Business," I just slipped outside, but this time I didn't budge. I was sixteen now, not ten or twelve or even fourteen, and I didn't see why I couldn't hear what Mom talked about.

"Bridget," Mom warned, her voice stern.

"Fine," I huffed loudly. "I'm sleeping over at Ann's, anyway."

I told Ann about what happened with Jimmy hitting Dad, and she insisted we look for him. We found him and Patrick at the edge of the campground in a lot that'd been cleared for building. There were piles of dirt all over and a mound of gravel right in the middle. Only there weren't any tractors or cranes or anything. Whoever was building whatever they were building had run out of money or given up.

Clouds had marched in and hung thick and low in the sky. A light breeze blew, and for the first time in days I wished I had a sweatshirt.

Jimmy and Patrick sat on a grassy spot on the corner of the lot. Next to Jimmy was a pile of stones, and he hurled them, one by one, out into the lot, but I couldn't figure out what he was trying to hit.

Ann eased down next to him. "Hey, are you okay?"

He didn't answer, and Patrick shot me a look that said Jimmy wasn't okay at all.

"All that money. They should've been proud," Ann said.

Jimmy nodded.

Ann continued, "I mean, look at everything you did—"

Jimmy cut her off. "All right. This isn't some big pity party, so lay off."

He jumped up and stalked off in the direction of the road. Ann ran after him, and Patrick and I followed. The three of us caught up with him, and we walked shoulder to shoulder, each waiting for someone else to break the silence. At the far end of the lot that bordered woods, we heard a rustling in the trees. I thought it was a deer, but then a man stepped out of the woods, straightening his shirt, and another man came out after him.

"Queers," Ann muttered, loud enough for them to hear. Like all of us, she'd been taught to hate them for it.

"Get the fuck out of here," Jimmy spat at them.

One of the men was skinny, and the other didn't look strong either. Jimmy and Patrick could easily take them. The skinny one, realizing this, held up his hands. "We don't want any trouble."

"Then get out of here," Jimmy threatened.

"Just leave them alone," Patrick said. "They're not bothering anybody."

"But they're queers," Ann said.

Jimmy turned from the men to Patrick. "What, are you a queer too?"

"Fuck off, Jimmy," Patrick said, raising his voice.

Jimmy stepped toward Patrick. "No, fuck you. You want to be next? I already broke my dad's nose. Want me to kick your ass too? Because I can, if that's what you want."

As Jimmy faced Patrick, the men hustled away.

"Would you stop?" I shouted at Jimmy and Patrick. "You're both being stupid."

Jimmy shook his head like Patrick wasn't worth bothering with. "Yeah, I'll stop," he said, and he turned and walked away.

"Shit," Patrick muttered.

Ann looked at me. "I'm going after him." She jogged in the direction Jimmy had gone, leaving Patrick and me alone.

I pulled out a pack of cigarettes and put one in my mouth, but before I could light it, Patrick grabbed it from me. He was practically the only Traveler I knew who hated smoking.

"Do you want to die?" he asked.

I felt the need to press his cautiousness, to test him again like I had at the swimming hole. "I don't know. Maybe."

"Well, I *do* know," he answered flatly. "I don't want you to for a good long time."

I sat down on the grass along the tree line, and Patrick eased down next to me. The clouds moved by fast, and the sky darkened. Rain, if it came, would still the red dust that covered everything—trailers, trucks, clothes, shoes—and made your skin gritty.

"Would you ever hit your dad?" I asked.

"Depends."

"Just would you?"

"Him and me get along. It's different."

I don't know why I was looking to Patrick for answers about what had happened with Dad and Jimmy. Like Patrick said, it was different. Patrick's father was different. Mr. Murphy spoke barely above a whisper and moved slowly and deliberately. He never yelled or acted on impulse. Jimmy said Mr. Murphy couldn't find his balls if his life depended on it. But even if Patrick had my dad for a father, I knew he would never hit him because Patrick was different too. He worked and played by the rules, and except for spending a little on his baseball cards, he didn't waste money or time on anything he didn't need.

"You wouldn't, I know you wouldn't," I told him.

"What does it matter, Bridget? Jimmy did, and he feels like shit about it."

"He said that?"

"Well, you know Jimmy. He wouldn't ever *say* that. But why do you think he was being such an ass?"

"It's funny, 'cause I thought I kind of wanted him to get in trouble. I mean, he's always getting away with everything. But now . . . You should have seen the look on Dad's face. I've never seen him look like that."

54

I turned from Patrick, remembering.

"Hey," he said, pulling a small brown paper bag from his pants pocket. "I've got something for you."

"What is it?"

"Just something. Go on, look inside."

Inside was a CD and a slip of paper, the receipt. Patrick had left it on purpose. Just like with his baseball cards, he'd paid for this legit. The CD was the Allman Brothers Band—*Eat a Peach*.

"I probably should've gotten you a book or something, but I'm not real good when it comes to picking out books. There's this song 'Melissa.' Have you ever heard it?"

I shook my head.

"It just reminds me of you, that's all. Listen to it and you'll see."

Patrick leaned toward me and we kissed. As we moved closer and closer to each other and Patrick pressed himself against me, I forgot about the *M* word. For the moment, Patrick was just my boyfriend. My sweet boyfriend who wanted me to quit smoking so I wouldn't die young and who gave me a CD with a song he said reminded him of me.

Patrick slid his hand under my shirt. I inched toward him, kissing him greedily. He felt over my bikini top and was working his way under when we heard Jimmy yell, "God, we can't leave you two alone for a minute."

Patrick took his hand away and slid off me.

"Let's go, Pat," Jimmy said.

Ann stood behind him and rolled her eyes, saying there was no getting through to Jimmy.

"Where?"

"I got an idea. Something that'll make us both feel better."

Ann and I didn't ask where they were going. And of course they didn't ask if we wanted to come. We knew the rules. But even though I knew the deal, it still hurt in the faraway place where I tucked my hopes. There, Jimmy's words still pounded and clawed at me, and I tried not to think about the girls Patrick would soon be talking to or messing around with.

Ann and I trailed Jimmy and Patrick back to the campground. Patrick turned to me once, as if he was trying to tell me something, but I looked away. I wouldn't let him see me hurting, see me caring about what he was doing. See me caring about him.

When we reached Jimmy's truck, Ann stopped. "See you later," she said more to Jimmy than to Patrick.

I kept walking. There was no way I was saying anything to Patrick—not even *Get lost and don't come back*. I don't know about Ann, but I listened to the motor of the truck as they pulled out. I listened until I couldn't hear it anymore.

That evening we munched pizza with Mrs. Murphy and watched a stupid TV movie about a mother searching for her kidnapped child. Mr. Murphy was out, probably at the same bar as Jimmy and Patrick. I wondered how Mrs. Murphy got used to it. Whether you just grew numb to it over time, and how long it would take me. If I ever could.

Mrs. Murphy was a tiny woman, only five foot two and maybe ninety pounds. She weighed more with all her heavy gold jewelry, though—thick bracelets and plaited necklaces and earrings that pulled on her earlobes. Mom said Travelers like Mrs. Murphy showed off their wealth that way. It was their way of saying *Look how great we're doing*. Just because she was small, though, didn't mean Mrs. Murphy was quiet like Mr. Murphy.

She skittered around and jabbered nonstop. Even while we were watching the movie, she filed her nails and talked to the TV. "Oh my God, she's gonna go and do that now? Oh my Lord! Honey, don't go and do that now!"

When the movie ended, Ann and I fled to the bunkroom she usually shared with Patrick. Since I was sleeping over, Patrick would sleep somewhere else—probably in Jimmy's truck, since they'd most likely be wasted anyhow. It wasn't a big deal. Now that they were older, Patrick and Jimmy slept somewhere else more often than they slept in their parents' trailers. Both of them, but especially Jimmy, were happy sleeping wherever they could roll up a sweatshirt or jacket for a pillow.

The bunkroom, like my bedroom and like every room in a trailer, was small, even with the sides popped out when you were parked. If you stood in the middle and held your hands out, you could practically touch the walls. Besides the bunks, one on top of the other, there was a small dresser. The walls had compartments for storing stuff, but other than that there was no room for anything else. Ann and I were used to it, just like we were used to having no privacy and keeping only the things we absolutely needed. But sometimes I wondered what it would be like to have a whole real room to myself. To have walls to plaster posters to, a big dresser to stand framed pictures on. A floor so big you could throw your clothes on one part and still have a part to walk on. A place where you could go and shut the door and feel away from the world. Where you could blast music or gab to your friends without worrying about someone overhearing.

"You tired?" Ann asked as I climbed up to the top bunk, Patrick's bunk.

"Not really."

Ann opened her dresser drawer and pulled out a bunch of magazines—*Seventeen, Cosmo, Glamour*. She handed me *Glamour* and took *Seventeen* for herself.

I was reading about the horrors of breast implants when Ann started reading out loud. "Listen to this. *The First Time: How to Make Yours Magical. A candlelit room, soft music playing in the background, fresh roses in a vase. Is this your dream of what your first time will be like? Well, if it is, you're not alone. It's the dream of thousands of teenage girls across America. Take Sherry—not her real name—a sophomore at Long Lakes High School in Long Lakes, Minnesota. 'I want more than doing it in the back of a car,' explains Sherry, sixteen. 'I want my first time to be special and something I'll remember forever.'* "

Ann read a few more sections out loud. The gist of the article was that girls shouldn't sit back and let their first time just happen. If they decided what they wanted and went after it, they could make it a magical moment.

"Some of those girls sound so stupid," I said. "I mean, as if candles and flowers are really important." To me it was more about loving and trusting the person you were with. But maybe that made those girls smart and *me* stupid. Candles and flowers came a lot easier than love and trust.

"Yeah, I know," Ann agreed. "But what do you think it'll be like?"

"I don't know."

"It's supposed to hurt."

"Yeah."

"Will you do it with Patrick before?"

"I don't know," I said shyly.

"Come on! Don't tell me you haven't thought about it."

Of course I had. Like all the time. "You know if my dad found out he'd kill us."

"I think I would with Jimmy," Ann confessed. "If he wanted to."

"You're not even engaged."

"I know."

"And you still would?"

"I think so."

I exhaled. "He's not worth it."

"You just think that because he's your brother."

It went beyond Jimmy being my brother. If it got around that Ann wasn't a virgin anymore, her chances for a good match would be ruined. I couldn't believe she'd even think of doing it with Jimmy if they weren't engaged. When I thought about doing it with Patrick, the thing that kept me from really wanting to wasn't so much Dad but whether Patrick really loved me. Ann didn't seem to care about Jimmy loving her.

As we fell asleep, I imagined my wedding in a way that I'd never been able to. Maybe Mom was right—Patrick would be a good husband and I'd come to love him. Maybe he'd just gone out with Jimmy because he knew Jimmy needed a friend right now. The way he'd taken Jimmy's shit over calling him a queer without Jimmy saying he was sorry showed that Patrick was a good friend. Maybe he didn't care about other girls. Plus, he had to go along or else he'd look like a loser in front of Jimmy and the other Traveler boys.

I saw myself dancing with Patrick and everyone circling us and clapping. And then I saw Patrick taking my hand and us going to the hotel. I played it out in my head, how we would go from kissing to having sex, making love, whatever you want to call it. My cousin Wanda had told me about her first time with Logan and how he got so tanked at the wedding reception that he passed out and they had to do it the next morning, when he had really bad morning breath. But our first time would be different. I imagined Patrick asking me if everything was okay, if it hurt. I imagined him caring about me, loving me.

That idea still trailed through my head when I woke in what seemed like the middle of the night to Jimmy's and Patrick's voices outside the trailer.

"What was her name?" Jimmy boomed, his words slurred.

Patrick laughed. His voice was loud too, louder than I'd ever heard him. "Jane? Joan? No, Jane, I think."

"Jane," Jimmy laughed. "Sweet Jane. You Jane, me Tarzan. Shit, she was hot."

I wasn't sure if Ann was awake, but how could she not be? They were practically yelling.

"What about your girl?" Jimmy asked. "She looked pretty tasty."

"Yeah," Patrick said.

"That's it? Come on! I want details."

"What can I say, I don't kiss and tell."

This sent Jimmy and Patrick into hysterics.

"I'm gonna piss my pants," Jimmy moaned.

Then Patrick—"Man, not right here, not right by the trailer"—and the hiss of Jimmy peeing on the pavement.

"Ann? You awake?" I whispered.

"Just go back to sleep, Bridget."

Even if I could have, it didn't matter because the door to the trailer opened. They were coming inside. I wished I was back in our trailer, anywhere but here as they came in drunk and probably smelling of some Country girl's perfume.

"They must think you're sleeping over at my place," I said.

As they opened the door to the bunkroom, Ann called, "Get out. We're in here."

This sent Patrick and Jimmy back into hysterics. "Sorree," Jimmy sang.

I listened to their voices as they left. Mr. and Mrs. Murphy didn't get up or say anything. Who knew if Mr. Murphy was even home yet, and Mrs. Murphy was used to this kind of thing, Patrick and Jimmy and Mr. Murphy coming home late and stumbling around. She knew exactly where they'd been and what they'd been doing and just didn't care anymore. Or pretended she didn't care anymore.

When it was quiet again, I waited for Ann to say something else. When she didn't, I huffed, "You still want to sleep with him?"

Ann didn't answer, and I remembered what she'd said about it not mattering what they did before they married, that it only mattered *who* they married. Maybe that was true—if they didn't rub your nose in it. If they kept quiet and it was easier to ignore. If you were a rock and didn't have feelings.

While Ann fell back asleep, I threw my covers off, hot with anger at what Patrick and Jimmy could do, what they were supposed to do, and what the rules were for me. After a few minutes, though, I shivered, suddenly freezing, thinking about Patrick with some other girl. The stupidest thing was I thought about him feeling her up like he would have me if Jimmy and Ann hadn't come back earlier that day. It was stupid because Patrick and whatever girl he'd been with had done so much more. They'd done everything. And I felt even stupider for imagining Patrick the way I had. Imagining our wedding night. If he loved me, how could he be with other girls? I pulled the covers over myself again and buried my face in the pillow, Patrick's pillow, trying to stop the tears that slid from the corners of my eyes.

chapter 7

Now that Jimmy was back we could finally set off again. During the next few weeks we logged a lot of time on the road—two-, three-, and four-lane highways and small, winding, one-lane, potholed back routes—rolling past fields of tobacco, corn, cotton, and hay, black-and-white cows and spotted horses grazing lush green pastures, and chain gangs in orange jumpsuits picking up soda cans and cigarette butts. We passed through town after tiny town. Towns with populations smaller than my grade back at St. Jude. Towns with crazy names like Eccentric, Alabama; Gas, Kansas; and Oddville, Kentucky.

We'd hit a town that'd been good for us last year and Dad and Patrick would spend a day or two working there. Then we'd pick up and move on. Sometimes Jimmy would even pitch in. Dad and Jimmy hadn't talked about their fight, at least not that I knew about. Like so often, instead of dealing with it, we ignored it. Only this time I wasn't sure we really could.

While the guys paved driveways and painted barns, Ann and I scammed the Kmarts and roamed the campgrounds. We went to yard sales to see if there was anything we could buy cheap and resell—a painting we could get for five dollars and then convince someone was worth a hundred. I picked up a few books, including a tattered copy of *The Diary of Anne Frank*.

I pretended things weren't different between Patrick and me, but the night Ann and I heard him and Jimmy changed everything. Mom must've noticed something different in me toward Patrick. I didn't smile when he joked with me, and I didn't wait on the steps of the trailer for him and Dad to come home in the evenings. When she asked me to help her make dinner one night in West Virginia, I knew she wanted to talk to me about him.

I used to help Mom make dinner all the time when I was younger. I'd stand on a step stool next to her at the counter so we'd be the same height. She'd give me my own little jobs, beating an egg or greasing a pan. Then she'd show me how to put the ingredients together and turn it all into a meal. I loved that time we spent together cooking and talking. I used to think how when I had a daughter of my own I'd be sure to teach her all the same recipes. But as I got older, I helped Mom less and less. I was always off with Ann or doing homework or reading, and we stopped cooking together. We stopped talking as much too.

That night's menu was spaghetti and meatballs. Mom molded the meatballs, and I stirred the two pots of spaghetti sauce—one regular and one called puttanesca, which Mom had torn the recipe for from *Country Cooking*.

"Is there anything you want to talk about?" Mom asked.

"Not really," I said.

"I mean, maybe something with Patrick? You seem like you've been kind of . . ." Mom glanced from the meatball cupped in her hand to me. "You seem kind of distant from him lately."

I don't know why I decided to say something close to the truth. I guess because it hurt so much I needed to share it with someone. I only hoped Mom cared enough about me to hear it—to really hear what I had to say.

"What would you say if I said I wasn't sure I wanted to marry Patrick?"

Mom answered right away. "I'd say every young girl's got nerves about getting married."

"But what if it's more than that?"

"It's not."

"How do you know?"

"Listen," Mom said. "You think I don't remember what it's like, but I do."

Fine. If Mom was so sure she knew everything, I'd put it all on the table. "Did Dad sleep around before you were married?"

"Bridget!" Mom slapped the meatball onto the counter, flattening it, and then, realizing what she'd just done, furiously set to remolding it.

"Well, did he?"

Mom cleared her throat. "That was none of my business."

"How was that not your business?"

"Because it wasn't—that's the way it is. Just don't think about those things and I promise you everything will work out fine."

This was not what I needed to hear. Mom wanted to talk, but she only wanted to talk about things her way. I wasn't letting her off so easy. "Does he sleep around now?" I pressed.

"Bridget," she warned sharply. "That's enough."

Mom glanced over at my sauce. I'd stopped stirring, and it

64

bubbled and hissed. "Sauce looks ready," she said, like nothing had just happened. Like she hadn't asked me to talk and then told me to shut up.

I didn't bother trying to reopen the conversation. Dad walked in, whistling, just as dinner was almost ready. He grabbed a beer from the fridge and popped the cap off using his hand and the side of the counter. The cap rattled on the counter and Dad picked it up and tossed it in the trash can. He leaned over the stove and said in a chipper voice, "Smells good, girls."

"You must have had a good day," Mom said.

"Not too bad, I guess."

Mom held a bowl out for me to put the spaghetti into. "Where's Jimmy?" she asked Dad.

Dad gulped his beer and wiped his mouth with the back of his hand. "How should I know? Haven't seen him all day."

Mom held her hand out for me to take the bowl back. "Why don't you go see if you can find him, honey," she said to me. "I'll finish putting dinner on the table."

"Hell no," Dad snapped. "Dinner's ready and we're eating, with or without him."

"Fine," Mom huffed, taking off her apron. I pulled my own apron over my head and carried the two sauces in their separate bowls to the table. I plopped down across from Jimmy's empty seat, the silverware and full glass of water, and wished for once Mom wouldn't set his place. But no, she couldn't ever stop because what if he came back and it was empty?

Dad forked a heap of noodles onto his plate.

"Now, there's two sauces," Mom explained. "A regular and a puttanesca."

Dad frowned. "Regular."

Mom ladled regular over his spaghetti. I'd planned on trying the puttanesca, but she hadn't answered my questions so I said, "I'll have the regular too."

Mom sucked in her lips and passed me the spoon to serve myself. Dad wolfed down most of his meal and then pushed his almost empty plate away. He held up his half-finished beer. "I have some news I think'll make you happy."

He didn't look at either of us in particular when he said it, and I wasn't sure who the news was supposed to make happy. When Mom shot him a look that said, *God, not now,* I was sure it wasn't going to make *me* happy.

"A toast," Dad said. "To Bridget and Patrick. April twenty-first."

I choked down my mouthful of meatball and looked from Dad to Mom.

"It's not set, Douglas," Mom said warily.

"It is. Shook hands with Tom this afternoon."

"Don't you think we should have—"

"There's no use waiting around. She's old enough, Mary."

Pure rage coursed through me. I couldn't believe it. They were talking like I wasn't even there. And if Dad was so set on matching someone up, it should've been Jimmy.

"It's settled and that's that," Dad declared. "I don't want to hear another word about it."

Dad *didn't* hear another word because I bolted. In that moment, my mind was freakishly clear. Without thinking of Mom or Dad or Jimmy or Patrick or of anybody but myself, I ran. I didn't care what Dad or Mom thought or what they'd do. I'd seen Jimmy bolt time and time again, but it'd never occurred to me to do it until now.

Dad called after me, but it was like I was underwater and

he was calling to me from above the surface. I heard his voice, but not his words. I ran out of the campground but didn't take the main road in case he came looking for me. I didn't know where I was going, but I was going somewhere. I took a side road, and after a few minutes I slowed to a brisk walk, trying to catch my breath. The road was narrow but straight, so people went sixty when the posted limit was forty-five. I stuck my thumb out to hitch, but the first three cars zoomed by, leaving me with only a gust of wind. I took down my ponytail and shook my head so my hair fell over my shoulders. I wished I was wearing something other than cutoffs and a tank top. But the next car stopped.

It was a truck, and I jumped in without looking at the driver. He could've been some complete sicko, a serial killer, but I didn't care. I'd only hitched a handful of times and never alone, but right then I felt like nothing could hurt me. Or maybe I was just hurting too much already for anything else to seep in.

When I did look, I saw the driver was a man in his forties with a thick mustache, receding hairline, and sad, small eyes. He wore blue overalls that said LARRY'S PLUMBING on the chest and FRED on the arm. His left hand on the steering wheel had no wedding ring, yet there was a picture of two kids clipped to the visor above him.

"I'm just going to Cedar Cove," he mumbled.

"Fine," I said. I had no idea where Cedar Cove was, but I didn't care. He could've said Kalamazoo and I would have said great.

It was a half-hour drive, and we were silent the whole way. I knew if I said just one word, he'd pour his life out to me. I didn't want to hear about the wife who had split, taking the kids and leaving him with nothing but an outdated picture and a job unclogging drains. I rolled down the window and leaned toward the rush of air. I thought of what I'd just done, how I'd just left them like that, and I felt like laughing and screaming at the same time. Screaming, *"I'm free!"*

I got out in Cedar Cove and headed for the town diner. I always carried money with me, no matter what. From the time I started wearing shoes, Mom told me to keep at least five bucks in my sock. This time I had seventeen dollars in my back pocket, which was enough to buy a grilled cheese and bacon, a Coke, and a coffee and still have plenty left over. The diner offered bottomless cups, so I sat there as the sun shot its fading purple and pink rays over the middle-of-nowhere town.

As people came and went, talking about the expected thunderstorms, my excitement faded. When I thought of Mom and Dad, I no longer felt like laughing or shrieking but instead worried over what they were thinking or doing. Every time the diner door opened, I turned, my heart quickening and my stomach jittering. When the waitress who'd been refilling my coffee pulled her apron over her head and touched up her lipstick using the edge of a knife as a mirror, I downed the rest of my coffee and left. I needed to find something to do—anything to wrench Mom and Dad from my head again.

I walked down the road leading out of town and stuck out my thumb again. The first car stopped—a black Mustang. This time, I looked at who was driving before I got in. I saw a guy not much older than Patrick or Jimmy. Short blond hair, thin lips, and tan skin. Khaki pants and a button-down shirt. He looked amazingly clean, like he'd never seen dirt in his whole life. Probably a college kid. Rich, or at least his parents were. The best thing about him, though, was that he looked like anything but a Traveler. He was just what I wanted. I climbed in and we sped off.

He turned his eyes from the road to me. "I'm Jared."

"Melissa," I said, thinking of Patrick's CD, which I'd thrown in the trash without even opening back in South Carolina—the day after I'd heard Patrick and Jimmy outside the trailer. Just using the name Melissa felt like some sort of revenge.

"From around here?" he asked.

"Back up the road a bit."

Jared nodded.

"How 'bout you?" I asked.

"My grandparents live on the golf course. I'm down here from up north for a few weeks. Shit, is this place boring." I didn't respond, and Jared said, "I didn't mean that as an insult, if you live around here."

I smiled. "No. It's boring. It sucks."

Jared took a hand from the wheel and rested it inches from mine. "So, where're you headed tonight?"

I looked at him. "I don't know. Where're you going?"

"I heard about this bar the next town over—Grady's? Thought I'd check it out."

"Sounds good to me," I said.

We flew on the back roads, Jared trying to impress me. I clutched the seat on the side farthest from him but didn't want him to slow down or stop taking his eyes off the road every now and then to glance at me. We passed signs for wildlife, and finally a sign welcomed us to the town of Belle Springs, population 557. Belle Springs looked like a million other out-of-the-way small Southern towns we'd driven through over the years. Squat houses with driveways and lawns full of rusting tools and dismembered cars. Dogs barking to be let in or howling to be let out. Run-down buildings and signs with letters missing from them. Even the sign for the bar was missing a letter—it read G ADY's instead of GRADY's. There must not have been another bar for miles because cars packed the lot.

I didn't have an ID, so I walked by the bouncer like I owned the place. I didn't look away because that would have done me in. I half smiled and kept right on going. Jared took out his wallet and seemed surprised that I was already on my way in. He caught up with me at the bar before I had a chance to order.

I let him buy me a Bud Light and with my back to the bar looked out over a pretty good crowd and a band covering Neil Young's "Cinnamon Girl." I'd been to plenty of bars before, usually with Mom or Dad, collecting some drunk cousin after a brawl. The dim lighting, the stale smell of beer and smoke and sweat, the throbbing music were familiar. Only tonight, it was all mine.

"Is this less boring?" I asked Jared. The music was so loud he didn't hear me, and I leaned over and said it again in his ear. Unlike Patrick's, his hair was cropped close to his neck. Even under his cologne, Patrick smelled musty, like gasoline and tar, but Jared didn't smell of anything but clean freshness.

"It's only less boring because of you," he said.

Maybe before, without three-quarters of a beer already downed, I would've looked away. But instead I stared back and then gulped the rest of the beer. I'd drunk beer plenty of times before, and harder stuff too. On Dad's lap when I was young, with Jimmy and Patrick and Ann, and at weddings and funerals. I didn't love its taste, but I knew the more I drank, the looser I'd feel. I hoped that invincible, incredible feeling would pump through me again. I hoped it could keep thoughts of Dad and Mom and Jimmy and Patrick away.

After two more beers, I weaved through the tangles of people to the bathroom. Halfway through the bar, I looked back. Jared was still there, right where I'd left him, and he was staring at me. Maybe it should have scared me. My insides did jump, but not in a bad way. I was still looking back at Jared when I felt a hand on my arm. I turned around to find myself face to face with Jimmy.

"Bridget? What the fuck?"

I looked for Patrick but didn't see him, and a surprising gush of relief rushed through me. Didn't I want Patrick to see me here? Wasn't that part of the point of coming? Getting even with him? Someone else was with Jimmy, though—a guy I'd never seen before. He had a goatee and wore cowboy boots—he was no Traveler. He jutted his chin toward me and said, "Who's this?"

"Go get another beer," Jimmy told him. "I'll take care of her."

The guy looked me over carefully before leaving. I stared back, trying to figure out who he could be and what Jimmy was doing with him. Maybe he was a Country guy Jimmy was talking to about a job. Sometimes Country folk could be trusted that way, although Dad never thought it was a good idea. Only this guy didn't give me the feeling he could be trusted at all. Dad's words ran through my head—*"You better not be selling."*

Jimmy waited until the guy was headed back to the bar and then said to me, "I don't know how you got here, but you better get home—now."

Jared had started toward us. I half wished he'd keep coming and half wished he wouldn't.

71

"Who the fuck's that?" Jimmy demanded when he saw him. "You fucking around with some Country guy?"

When he reached us, Jared moved between Jimmy and me. "Hey, man, what's the problem?"

"I don't know who the fuck you are, but you better back off," Jimmy warned.

With Jimmy's attention on Jared, I turned and took off. I pushed through the crowd, spilling people's drinks, and flew past the bouncer to the parking lot. Outside, it was still warm and muggy, but at least it wasn't smoky. My head and stomach were spinning. I looked behind me to make sure Jimmy wasn't following and then cradled my head in my hands to make the world slow down.

I started when Jared came up behind me.

"It's just me," he said. "Who is that guy?"

"Nobody. I gotta get out of here."

"Come on," Jared said, reaching for my hand.

We drove to a pond that Jared said he'd been waterskiing on when he was younger. I thought of the swimming hole Patrick and Ann and I'd gone to—how Patrick had been so cautious. What would he think of me now? There were no other cars in the small, sandy lot. Jared killed the engine, and through the open windows, I could hear the tree frogs chirping.

He turned to me. "How old are you anyway?"

"Eighteen."

Jared sighed. "I wasn't sure if you were a lot younger."

"Nope. I'm almost nineteen, actually. My nana says when I'm her age it'll be good to look young."

"Does your nana live with you or something?"

"Actually, I live with her," I said, making my story up just then. "My parents died in a car wreck when I was ten."

72

"God," Jared breathed. "I'm really sorry."

I looked straight at him, feeling comfort in the lies that came so easily to me. "Did you kill them?"

Jared furrowed his brow. "No."

"Then don't be sorry."

He let out a quick laugh. "You're tough, Melissa. You're not like the girls I'm used to."

"Is that bad?" I asked.

Jared shook his head. "I think it's good."

With his hand on my chin, Jared turned my face toward his. The first kiss was soft, barely grazing my lips. Then they came harder, deeper, like Patrick's but sloppier, wetting not just my lips but the skin around them too. It was a different sort of kissing. With Patrick it was like he wanted *me*. With Jared, it felt like he just wanted someone. It was like I could be anybody. But at first that strong desire, even if it wasn't for me in particular, infected me too. I kissed him back and waited for him to move his hand up my shirt. After what Patrick had done, I wanted someone else to be the first to really touch me there. I wanted that revenge. But Jared didn't go up my shirt. Instead he wrestled with the button and zipper on my shorts. My mind froze, and any desire I had dropped away. My lips stopped moving, but Jared didn't seem to notice as he wrestled my cut-offs halfway down my legs.

He pulled a lever on the side of the seat. It tilted back and he climbed on top of me. Every muscle in my body tightened, but again Jared didn't notice or didn't care. I made a fist and pressed my fingernails into my own skin as hard as I could, hoping to feel something, but I still barely registered the pain. My heart was slamming so hard against my chest that I didn't know how Jared couldn't hear it. I knew what was happening, and as much as I wanted to hurt everyone—Mom, Dad, Patrick—I didn't want my first time to be like this, like those girls in the article who regretted their first time but only worse. I heard myself saying, *Wait, hold on, stop,* but it was only in my head. My throat felt swollen and blocked. I finally moved my hand to Jared's chest but I found no strength to push him away. Jared worked his hand down my underwear and I gasped, but he didn't stop and I still didn't try to stop him.

Then someone yanked open the door. At first I thought it was the cops, and for once the thought of the cops was a good thing. I was just glad something, someone, had stopped what I couldn't. But when I saw who it was, I wished it was the cops more than ever.

chapter 8

Jimmy reached into the car, tore Jared out, and swung once, knocking him against the hood. Then he grabbed me and threw me onto the ground. I broke my fall with my outstretched hands, but my face still hit the ground and I tasted dirt. I spat and wriggled my shorts back up over my hips as Jimmy yelled at me to get over to his truck.

Jared pulled himself off the hood, and before he could take a swing or maybe run, Jimmy bashed him again. Jared's head lolled back like his neck muscles had given out. Next Jimmy blasted him in the stomach, and blood spurted from his mouth. He rolled onto the ground and Jimmy booted him in the ribs.

"Jimmy!" I yelled. Tears leaked from my eyes and my whole body trembled. I wanted to tell him to let Jared be. That he'd done enough. I wanted to tell him that I hadn't said no. That Jared might've stopped if I had. That I was stupid for looking for something from Jared that he could never give me. But it was all I could do to keep from sobbing, and everything was happening so fast. And maybe I was just glad someone was taking control.

Jimmy looked at me fiercely. "Get over to the truck, now!"

I ran to the truck and climbed in. Before I shut the door, I heard a few more of Jimmy's punches, or maybe they were kicks. I winced at each blow. Then I heard Jared groan. That groan was the worst—the way it was something that'd escaped from him involuntarily. I knew Jimmy was beating Jared so badly he might die. All because of me. All because I was stupid enough to think I could run away and escape. Because I was stupid enough to think I could do what he and Patrick did.

I looked at the sky, clear and full of bright stars, and tried not to think about what Jimmy was doing to Jared. I remembered how when Jimmy and I were young, Dad told us stories about our ancestors back in the Middle Ages who traveled the land repairing weapons and later pots and pans. They used the constellations to know when to move on and where to go. Dad taught us the same constellations. Even now, I could pick out Orion, the Big and Little Dippers, and my favorite, the Seven Sisters. Dad told us how our people came from Ireland to America during the Potato Famine, when everyone was starving. How they traveled here, making a living any way they could—trading horses, selling fake lace, and working scams. How they held on to their heritage in this new country by never giving up their lifestyle, by never marrying out of the clan, and by putting family above everything else. Sometimes it was hard to believe we came from those people at all.

Jimmy came back to the truck, his shirt splattered with blood. He opened the passenger door and yanked me out by my arm. Then he slapped me so hard my jaw rocked.

"What the fuck did you think you were doing?" he screamed.

I didn't answer. I was crying harder now and shaking.

"You know what he called you? You know what he said back in the bar when you left? He said, 'What do you want with that white trash anyway?'" Jimmy shook his head in complete disgust. "You're just lucky Patrick ain't here to see this."

People called us lots of things—gypsies, con artists, thieves, swindlers, even trailer trash. But still, Jimmy's words—Jared's words—cut me in a way those names didn't anymore. It was different when people said it about us. Jared was saying it about *me*.

I held back my tears as best I could, but I still trembled as we drove back to the campground. My window was open, and the air blew my hair across my face. I hoped the wind would erase Jimmy's slap, which still burned fresh and raw.

Jimmy stopped the truck a little ways from our trailer. He reached out for me and I winced, thinking he might hit me again. But he wiped a few of my escaped tears away with his fingers. My body softened and the tears rushed back full force.

"Tell Mom and Dad I had to take off," he said.

"What do I say when they ask why?" I managed to ask.

"Tell them I just had to, that's all."

I nodded. If they hadn't already, someone would find Jared in a few hours. If he was alive and could talk, they'd come looking for Jimmy. Or maybe someone had seen something. On top of everything else now, because of me, Jimmy was in trouble.

"See you down the road, though, right?" I said. I couldn't handle the thought of him leaving—not because of this. Not because of me.

"Dad said Greensboro. I'll be there."

* * *

I eased open the door to the trailer, even though no lights were on. Inside, I felt my way to my room by memory. I lay down on my bed, fully dressed and still shaking. I breathed in and out, trying to calm down. It was over. Dad snored in the other room, and I wondered what he and Mom had done after I'd left. Had Dad looked for me? Had Mom cried? If I coughed now, turned on a light, would they get up? Or would they just say, *"She's home,"* roll over, and fall back asleep? I wanted to know, but I couldn't face them—not yet.

I didn't change out of my clothes but stayed facedown on my bed. I closed my eyes and buried my face in the pillow, wishing it would all go away, wishing none of it had ever happened. Usually I could sleep no matter what—with the TV blaring in the living room or with people yelling outside. If I woke up, I'd turn over and be out again in minutes. But sleep wouldn't come. I didn't want to think about Jared, but it was impossible not to. I saw him kissing me, clawing into my underwear, then saw the blood spurting from his mouth. I clutched my stomach, gagged, and tasted beer mixed with panic and regret. And what if Jimmy hadn't come? Where would I be now? My face burned as I imagined Jared ripping down my underwear, pushing himself inside me. Would I finally have stopped him? Would he have stopped? Would I have yelled, kicked, clawed? Or would I have just let it happen?

I was still awake when the sun rose over the nearby road. Trucks whooshed by on the highway; Mom and Dad's alarm clock buzzed; the toaster dinged. The smell of coffee on the stove drifted in. I lay still, growing hot under the covers, listening to Mom and Dad.

"Gonna go find Jimmy," Dad said.

"Douglas," Mom said. "You'll go looking for her, right?"

"If Jimmy doesn't know anything, yes."

The screen door opened and closed. I pictured Mom with the tired look on her face I'd seen a hundred times before when Jimmy took off. Hearing them, not angry but only worried, I climbed out of bed. My jaw ached from where Jimmy'd hit me.

I opened the door slowly, my stomach thrashing at what Mom would do when she saw me. She turned right away. "Bridget! We didn't know where you'd gone. That was so unlike you to run off like that. What's gotten into you?" Mom hugged me, but I pulled away, all of my sympathy for her, my guilt over making her worry, suddenly gone.

"Jimmy takes off all the time," I said. After everything that had happened, it shouldn't have mattered that Mom and Dad expected it from Jimmy but not from me. But it did.

"Jimmy can take care of himself," Mom said.

"And I can't?"

Mom and Dad had always taught me to look out for myself. I stole, went along on roofing and driveway jobs, and helped Mom sell trailers before I had learned the alphabet or how to tie my shoes. I was grown-up enough to do all that but not to make decisions about my own life?

"We were just worried. You know Jimmy, but you . . ." Mom paused and ran her eyes up and down me, taking in the dirt on my knees and my untucked tank top. She stepped toward me again and reached out for my cheek, concern growing in her eyes. "What happened? Your face . . .?"

I forced back the tears. I wanted to let everything out. I wanted to tell Mom about Jared and about Jimmy beating him. About Jimmy hitting me. But she'd freak and tell Dad. And Jimmy had only been protecting me. He hadn't made me swear not to tell, but I'd known what he meant when he said, *"Tell Mom and Dad I had to take off."* That was *all* I was supposed to tell them.

When I didn't answer her, Mom said, "Did Patrick do this? Because if he—"

I shook my head. "No."

"Who was it, then?"

"No one. It was me. I was running and it was dark and I tripped."

Mom sighed. "Where's Jimmy?"

"He left," I said. "He had to. Said he'd meet us in Greensboro."

Mom reached for me again, and this time I let her touch my cheek before I dropped my head and stared at the ground. Her voice was soft but clear: "You better clean up before your father gets back."

I thought about refusing to change, making Dad see a different side of me. But it was too late for proving a point. Things had spun out of control, and the best thing would be to try to go back to normal. Even though I hated to admit it, Mom was right. Dad couldn't see me like this.

I took a shower and let the warm water run over me. There was only so much water in the tank, so showers usually had to be short, but I stayed a long time, hoping the water could scald me clean of Jared and the whole night. But then it turned luke-warm and I shivered. I got out, toweled off, and put on warm clothes even though it was hot out—jeans and an oversize I LOVE NY sweatshirt Big Jim had given me years ago. But I still couldn't shake the damp, cold feeling. The feeling that nothing would ever be right again.

In my room I looked in the mirror. My cheek was red and

blotchy from where Jimmy had slapped me, and there was a scratch too, probably from when he'd thrown me to the ground. But it was nothing I couldn't cover with a little makeup. I turned away. Looking into the mirror was like hearing my own voice on a recording—what I saw staring back at me seemed off. I didn't know myself anymore, didn't want to know myself.

Dad stomped back into the trailer. "No sign of him."

"She's back," Mom said. "She must've come home after we fell asleep. She's in her room."

I waited for Dad to ask Mom where I'd been. For him to yell, *"Bridget, get out here, now!"* I didn't know what Mom told him with her expression, but his only reply was, "Good." And then, "Can't find Jimmy." I was glad he didn't want to talk to me, but at the same time it stung. He just wanted to forget the whole thing and hope it never happened again.

"I'm sure Jimmy's still out looking for her," Mom said.

"Yeah, well, somebody has to make some money around here," Dad grumbled. "I'm gonna go get Patrick."

At the thought of Patrick my stomach curled again. Because of what he'd done weeks before, but more because of what I'd just done. I'd thought I was so cool. That I could do what he did. That I could get back at him. I'd thought I had power, running away, latching on to Jared. I'd imagined things were different in the real world. But in fact, nothing was different at all. Maybe I hadn't stopped Jared because I'd realized something right then—that it didn't matter what I did. Things would happen to me even if I didn't want them to. Maybe Dad and Mom were right. I'd be lucky to have Patrick to take care of me. Because I couldn't take care of myself.

I took a brush to my hair. It hurt as I ripped out the knots and I pulled harder. Punishing myself for ever thinking I could choose. For being so dumb. For letting Jimmy see me like he did, with my shorts around my knees, Jared on top of me. And for making him run.

Dad and Patrick came back a few minutes later. I listened as they filled the tanks on the truck. They used really cheap roof and driveway sealer, and then they mixed it with so much water that it didn't work for shit. They added a bit of aluminum paste, which made the color right, but the aluminum didn't do much either. The roofs and driveways looked good at first, but it washed off in a few months or when the first hard rain came. But by that time, we were always long gone.

When they finished, Dad said, "All set?"

"One sec," Patrick said. The trailer door yawned open and Patrick was right outside my door. "Morning, Mrs. Daugherty."

Mom sounded fed up. "She's not feeling well, Patrick."

"Can I see her just for a second?"

I put my hairbrush down and quietly climbed back under the covers. I held my breath and prayed that Mom would say no. What would I do if he opened that door? What would I say?

"She's sleeping," Mom said. "When you get back."

I thought I could hear Patrick's breathing, but I knew I was imagining it. Trailer walls are thin, but not that thin. I wondered if he'd argue with Mom, demand to see me. *Please, Pat, just go away,* I thought. *For your own good, go away.*

"Tell her I hope she feels better," he said, and the trailer door slapped shut. Then the truck door opened and slammed, the engine turned over, and the wheels crunched on the ground as Patrick and Dad pulled away. I closed my eyes, just wanting a minute to not think. I was even hoping to drift off to sleep, to somehow find a way out of the mess I'd caused, but Mom knocked softly on my door.

"Come in," I managed.

She carried a plate of toast. When I didn't take it, she put it on the little side table next to my bed. "You should eat something."

Tears welled at the corners of my eyes.

"Should I try again?" Mom asked.

I shook my head, wanting her to leave me alone but also wishing she'd pester me until I told her everything.

"You can't tell me much of anything, can you?"

"No," I said. "I'm sorry."

Mom sighed. "Patrick came around last night too."

"What did you tell him?"

"The truth. That you ran off and we didn't know why."

"You knew why."

Mom closed her eyes and inhaled deeply. "If you don't marry him, it'll be somebody else. You're scared. I know that. But you'll get married, start your own life, have your own kids. . . ."

Mom was right—after marrying Patrick, my whole life would fall into place. Traveling, selling trailers, working Wal-Marts, counting money. Then having kids of my own and teaching them our life. Nothing would ever be different. *That* was what I was scared of. I didn't want her life.

"Go to sleep now," Mom said, her voice soft. "Later you'll talk to Patrick."

This time I did sleep. A hungry sleep without dreams that I was grateful for. I knew that for a long time Jared's groping hands and bloody face would fill my dreams.

The ring of Mom's cell phone woke me. I came out of what

felt like a great deep blackness, and it took me a minute to know where I was.

"Can't talk now. Call you later."

Mom's words spun in my head as sleep let go of me. I climbed out of bed and found her flipping through *Cooking Light*.

"Who was that?" I asked.

"Just business."

Business. The business I was too young for Mom and Dad to tell me about even though I was old enough for them to marry me off. "Don't you think it's time you started talking about business stuff in front of me?" I asked Mom. "I mean, if I'm about to be married."

"Not now, Bridget," Mom said.

"But how am I gonna do the books and that kind of stuff if I don't learn?"

Mom sighed. "Just not right now . . . not after everything that's happened."

"Fine," I said. I didn't have the will to fight her about it.

I was sitting outside the trailer when Dad and Patrick rolled in that afternoon. Black from the sealant covered their hands and shirts. There was a spot on Patrick's cheek too, and it stood out against his skin. I had slathered on some foundation, covering my own stain.

"Good day?" I asked, looking at Dad and avoiding Patrick's gaze.

"Not bad." Dad shrugged and went inside. Dad and I would act just like he and Jimmy did after their fight—we'd pretend nothing had happened and everything was fine.

With Dad gone, I had to look at Patrick. For a second,

when we first looked at each other, I wondered if *we* would pretend nothing had happened too. But then Patrick narrowed his eyes. "Where were you?"

The anger I'd felt in the Murphys' trailer listening to him and Jimmy talk roared up again. "Why do you care?"

"What's that supposed to mean?"

"You know what it means."

"No, I don't." Patrick grabbed my hand and eyed the trailer, telling me with his look that we needed to talk and right here was not the place. "Come on."

I shook off his grasp but followed. I wasn't sure what we'd say to each other, but we couldn't go on like this. We passed Whitey Costello's trailer and the Murphys', silent as we walked, looking for a place where no one would hear us. Right now we cared, but I imagined that in a few years, once Patrick and I were married, we would yell and scream outside our trailer like it was nothing.

A chain-link fence marked the back edge of the campground. I leaned up against it and Patrick hovered close. Usually his eyes were wide and kind, open, like you could see all of him in them, but right then they were narrowed slits.

"What's this all about?" he demanded.

"You get to screw around. Why can't I?"

Patrick's face tensed. He said in a voice that was strong but trembling, a voice I'd never heard him use, "So that's what you were doing? Screwing around?"

"Yeah, so call off the wedding, why don't you? Tell your dad you don't want to marry me."

"Is that what you want?" he asked.

I dropped my eyes to my feet. I heard Mom's voice in my head. *"If you don't marry him, it'll be somebody else."*

"I don't know what I want," I mumbled. It was true. So

pathetically true. I had no idea what I wanted from my life or from Patrick. Each time I thought I knew, everything changed and I didn't know again.

Patrick stepped closer to me, his warm breath on my face. His voice was softer now. "Did you listen to that song?"

I shook my head. "I heard you and Jimmy that night. I heard you talking about those Country girls. Ann and I both did." I didn't want him to know that it mattered—that I cared—but it still hurt too much to say nothing.

Patrick didn't answer, and maybe I didn't want him to. What was he supposed to do? Lie and say it hadn't happened?

"What went down last night?" he asked. "Where's Jimmy?"

"He beat up some Country boy and had to take off."

" 'Cause of you?"

I nodded.

"What'd you two do?"

He meant me and the Country boy. Not me and Jimmy. As much as I wanted to hurt him, I couldn't tell him. And even though I wasn't sure I wanted to marry him, I also knew I didn't want to lose him. "Nothing," I said.

It was the truth, really. Jared and I'd kissed; he'd climbed on top of me, clawed his hand down my shorts. But that was it, even though it felt like so much more. And when it came down to it, it wasn't anything I'd wanted. It was just something I'd thought I'd needed to get back at him.

"Nothing?" Patrick asked.

"Nothing."

Patrick sighed and pulled me to him, whispered in my ear, "Bridget, don't scare me."

I didn't know if he meant I scared him because I ran away or because I might've been with someone else. But either way, he believed me. He believed that nothing had happened. Or else he just didn't want to think about it. Maybe he did know the truth deep down—that *something* had happened. Like I knew the truth about him sleeping with other girls but didn't want to face it.

After that night, I wanted to believe in Patrick a little. Believe that he could make me happy somehow and that maybe he wanted the same from me. Maybe we wanted to believe in each other. I clung to him and inhaled the familiar mix of sealant and sweat. Patrick was a good head taller than me, and I buried my face in his chest. He didn't let go, but held me tighter.

chapter 9

Every day before we left for Greensboro, I flipped through the local paper at the campground office. I braced myself as I turned each page, scanning for a headline that read *Man Beaten to Death* or *Suspect Sought in Savage Beating*. But there was nothing in the police notes or anywhere else. Somehow, Jared had lived.

When we finally left, it wasn't because the work dried up but because rain threatened. The sticky humidity of the morning turned into early-afternoon clouds the color of the Smith and Wesson Dad kept in his top dresser drawer. At the first rumbles and groans the sky belched up, Dad and Patrick came home. Mr. Murphy followed soon after. He drove right on up to our trailer and joined Dad and Patrick in looking at the sky.

"Think it's gonna pass on through?" Mr. Murphy asked Dad.

Dad squinted at the thick clouds. "I don't know."

Over the last few days, they'd paved driveway after driveway and done a few roofs too. If the storm brought mostly noise and little rain, their work would stand. But if it blasted like thunderstorms and lightning storms usually did down south, black water would gush through the streets. Once people figured out they'd been swindled, some of them might go to the cops. A lot of people wouldn't ever tell anyone, though, because that meant admitting they'd been stupid enough to pay two men who knocked on their door offering their services. That was why we got away with most of what we did—because people's pride kept them from telling. But you never knew when someone *would* tell, and Dad's usual policy was better safe than sorry.

"Think we should wait it out?" Mr. Murphy asked.

Dad clucked and then shook his head. "Let's get on."

"All right," Mr. Murphy said. "It's your call."

Dad usually called the shots, in part because Patrick was joining our family, but also because Dad was the one who usually had the opinions.

We hooked up the trailer, and as we pulled out of the campground and turned onto the highway, and Plainville and then Cedar Cove and Belle Springs slipped away, I let out a breath I'd been holding since Jimmy's first punch had landed. I tried to let everything that had happened slip away too. Jared hadn't died, so I told myself to forget all about him and Belle Springs. Even though deep down I knew forgetting wouldn't come so easily, the sight of the black pavement spreading out behind us like an oil spill made me think maybe it could.

It poured. Rain slapped the windshield, and even at full speed the wipers couldn't keep up. We had to slow down to thirty, and it took us an extra hour to get to Greensboro. But by the time we rolled into the campground, the sky had cleared again and it was lighter than when we'd left Plainville.

I was outside with Dad unhooking the trailer when Jimmy

strode toward us. Someone was with him, and I could tell from the hulking walk and bushy brown hair that it was Big Jim. When they were only a few feet away, Jimmy announced, "Look who I found."

I didn't know if Jimmy or Big Jim heard him, but at the sight of Big Jim, Dad murmured, *"Christ."*

Jimmy wore the world's biggest grin; it was no secret he worshiped Big Jim. He loved the fact that he was named after him, since Big Jim was practically a legend among the Northern Travelers for the scores he'd pulled off over the years. It was customary among our people for one brother to name his kid after the other brother. But ever since Big Jim and Dad's blowup fight, Dad said he wished he'd never named Jimmy after him.

Big Jim slung his arm around me first, before even looking at Dad. He hugged me so tight it hurt, and I wriggled away. Big Jim got his nickname long before Jimmy was born because he was six feet four and solid as a telephone pole, not necessarily muscled or fit, but just plain big. Since so many of us shared the same last names and even the same first names, nicknames were common: Whitey, Mikey Boy, Big Jim. Country folk thought we were strange to keep using the same names, but it was hard to track down one particular James Sullivan when there were six of them at the same campground.

Sometimes Big Jim had a thick brown beard that matched his overgrown eyebrows, but now he had only a covering of dark stubble. "Look at Bridget," he said. "All grown up."

Big Jim and Dad shook hands, and I thought back to the last time we'd seen Big Jim. It was a few years ago at the spring burials, the year we buried Pop, Dad and Big Jim's father. Even though most Northern Travelers wintered in some part of Florida, they scattered all over during the summer months, and so when our people passed away we didn't always bury them right off. We kept their bodies on ice at funeral homes, and twice a year, spring and fall, everyone came for one big funeral. Those were the times for weddings too. All the cousins and second cousins and even people who were only somewhat related and we hadn't seen in forever showed up to bury Pop. Big Jim and Dad pretended everything was fine, but after too many beers, they ended up screaming at each other and nearly throwing punches again.

"Jim," Dad grumbled. "Didn't know you were gonna be in the area."

Big Jim smiled. "It was fate. I was coming to look for you all and in drives Jimmy."

Dad cranked the trailer up on its wheel. "Go on and see Mary." He nodded to the trailer. "I'll be right in after I finish up here."

Big Jim looked at Jimmy and clapped him on the back. "You just gonna stand there? Finish up for your old man so we can go on inside."

Jimmy stepped forward and reached for the hitch crank. "I got it," he said to Dad.

Dad hesitated, eyeing Jimmy like he didn't even trust him with the hitch. But then he turned and headed inside. Big Jim followed Dad, and I followed Big Jim.

"Jim's here," Dad called to Mom as we came inside.

"Big Jim?" Mom's tone was one of surprise mixed with worry.

"The one and only," Big Jim chuckled.

Mom smiled faintly. She hugged Big Jim loosely and then went to the fridge and came back with two beers. She handed one to Big Jim and one to Dad.

Big Jim took the beer and sat down on the couch. Dad eased into his recliner, pulling the lever so the bottom popped out and he could put his feet up. Mom stayed in the kitchen and so did I, standing with my back against the stove. With Dad and Big Jim in the same room, access to an exit was always a good idea.

"So, Douglas," Big Jim said. "How's the work?"

Dad nodded. "Good enough."

"Pulling in good numbers?"

"Just fine."

"Jimmy tells me it's been a little slow."

"That's funny," Dad said, not laughing in the slightest. "Jimmy ain't been working much. . . . I don't know how he'd know."

"Well, either way, I was looking to find y'all because something big's going down. Something I know you're gonna want to be in on."

Mom eyed Dad from across the room. "I don't know if we're really looking for anything."

"You're gonna want to hear this one, Mary," Big Jim said.

"Go on," Dad told him. He nodded to Mom. "Hear him out."

I began to think maybe things had changed between Dad and Big Jim, that the last few years apart had made them hate each other less.

"Well," Big Jim began. "Like I said, this one's gonna be big."

While Big Jim explained the job, Jimmy came inside, wiping the grease from the hitch onto his jeans. Mom looked at him with soft eyes and a curl of the lips that said, *You're back and you're okay*. Jimmy granted her a smile and went to the fridge, grabbed a beer, and stood near me in the kitchen as Big Jim continued. Big Jim laid it all out for us, and I realized that everything Jimmy gushed about was true—not only were Big Jim's scams huge, but he was good at them.

"It's easy . . . in and out," he said when he was done explaining how it'd work. "I figure we'll make at least a hundred *kade*."

"What about this Country guy?" Dad asked. "Don't tell me he's doing this for free."

The whole scam hinged on a Country person Big Jim knew. Dad didn't trust any Country folk and always said Big Jim was asking for trouble working with them.

"He gets ten percent," Big Jim answered.

"So it's ninety, not a hundred," Dad said.

"You can have the fifty," Big Jim promised. "I'll take forty. It's solid. I checked out all the angles."

"Arizona's a long way to go for it not to come through," Dad said. "And while we're there, we'd be losing the steady cash we'd be making here."

Big Jim nodded. "That's the risk. The risk for the big payoff."

"So why do you need us?"

"I figure we need at least one person besides me to make it look professional. We could also use Bridget to answer the phones. How 'bout it, brother, you in? Me, you, and Bridge—it'd be a hell of a lot of fun."

Dad shook his head. "I'm not going."

Jimmy stepped forward. "I'll go."

"I don't know about all this," Mom stammered. I knew she was thinking about more than losing money; she was thinking of us getting busted.

"I can handle it," Jimmy said.

Dad glared at Jimmy. "I didn't say you were going."

"God, Dad," Jimmy cried. "Did you hear him? One hundred *kade*. One hundred *kade*!"

"It's ninety *kade*, and we only get fifty of it—*if* everything goes the way Jim says."

Jimmy looked at Big Jim. "See? This is what I'm talking about. This is what I mean."

Big Jim raised a hand and silenced Jimmy. "Go on outside and let me talk to my brother. Bridget, you go on too."

I was happy enough to leave, but Jimmy stomped out and let the screen door snap behind him. Outside, he said, "If they don't let me go, I swear I'll . . ."

"You'll what?"

"Leave, I guess."

Jimmy took a swig of his beer. He sat on the bumper of Dad's truck, and I eased down next to him. I looked at the moon rising to its highest perch in the sky, and it was nice sitting there with Jimmy, not fighting or hating each other, just talking. I'd thought Jimmy and I would never come together, would never be friends. I'd thought I hated him. But I was coming to see what our life was like for him too. In some ways we were more alike than I'd thought. He wanted control of his life just like I did mine.

"Thank you," I said softly.

"For what?"

"You know. . . ."

"Don't talk about it," Jimmy warned. "Don't you ever talk about it again."

I swallowed, nodded. I sensed Jimmy wasn't ashamed of me or what had happened but just wanted to make it easier on me, to give me the chance to forget. We sat and listened to what we

94

could hear from the trailer. At first it was just mumbling. Then the voices grew louder.

"You don't come in here like you're some cowboy," Dad yelled. "Fucking John Wayne. Rambo."

"You still don't get it, do you?" Big Jim boomed. "Still playing in the sandbox."

"How would my family live if I was like you? If I was in and out of the *quad*? Wanted in five states? Or is it six now? What number you up to these days? Pop would be so proud—God rest his soul."

"You haven't changed. I thought now the kids were older you'd quit using them as a damn excuse. But it's no different. I see that."

"Get out of my house," Dad ordered.

"It's a trailer," Big Jim scoffed. "You're a Traveler, remember?"

"I think you're the one who's forgotten," Dad scolded him. "Don't you remember what Pop taught us? Not to go for any old shot in the dark?"

"And where'd it get him?" Big Jim asked. "Didn't even leave us enough money to pay for his plot."

The door opened and Big Jim strode out.

"You're a goddamn *yonk*," Dad called after him, using the Cant word for a Traveler who forgot the rules of the clan.

Jimmy jumped up from the truck bumper. "I told you."

Big Jim ignored him and sat down next to me. The front end of the truck sank under his weight. He spoke calmly, like nothing had happened. "So I hear you're headed to the altar, Bridget."

"Yeah, I guess so."

"Marriage." Big Jim chuckled. "I wish I could give you some kind of advice."

Big Jim had married a Country girl who converted to a

Traveler. Converting was practically unheard of, not because Country folk weren't willing to but because Travelers shunned those who mixed with Country blood. I didn't remember Big Jim's wife well because I was pretty young when they divorced. Mom says it was the only time Travelers approved of a divorce, both because Lenora was Country and because she was a bitch. Everyone was grateful that they never had any kids, and it made the divorce easier too. But by the way he acted around me and Jimmy, sometimes I wondered if Big Jim wished they had.

"If I were your daughter, would you make me get married?" I asked.

"That mean you don't want to?"

I shrugged.

"I don't know the first thing about kids. Your father does a good job raising you two. You wouldn't want to know what you'd turn out to be if you were raised by someone like me."

"We'd be better," Jimmy said. "I know it."

Big Jim halted Jimmy with a look. "Don't go talking bad about your father. Ever. Not to me or anyone."

"But you heard him for yourself," Jimmy said.

Big Jim stared at Jimmy sternly. "I warned you once. This last time is a gift."

Jimmy sighed and eased down next to Big Jim. It didn't make sense to him how Big Jim could act like he did to Dad and then come out here and defend him to us. But I could understand it a little. Like how I said I didn't want to marry Patrick and then there I was in his arms and never wanting to let go.

"I just want to go with you," Jimmy said. "That's all."

Big Jim heaved one arm around Jimmy and the other around me. "I know. I know you do."

chapter 10

I was reading on the couch, minding my own business, passing time while we waited for Dad to decide about Arizona. Mom was hanging clothes on the line. Her cell rang, and I saw that she'd left it sitting on the kitchen counter. Without thinking much about it I jumped up and grabbed it.

Through the window I saw that Mom had heard the ringing and was now on her way into the trailer. There I was, holding her phone, something I wasn't supposed to do. There was plenty of time for me to put it back down and pretend to be getting something from the fridge, but instead I glanced at the face of the phone to see who was calling. The area code was 617 and the name under the number was Russell Berger.

When Mom opened the door and saw me with the phone, she rushed at me. "Bridget!" she cried, and snatched the phone. She looked at who was calling but didn't answer.

"Why aren't you picking up?" I asked.

"That's none of your business," she snapped.

"Right. Of course it's none of my business. My own life isn't my business, so why should some phone call be."

I stormed out of the trailer and walked around the campground for a few minutes to cool off, but thinking about what had just happened got me more worked up. Why was Mom being such a freak about me listening to her phone calls? And why hadn't she at least answered and then either gone outside to talk, asked me to leave, or called the person back?

Then it hit me. Maybe it wasn't business she didn't want me to hear but something else. Maybe she was talking to one of the advisors about Jimmy. Advisors were Travelers who didn't go on the road anymore. Usually they were older or sick, and so they stayed in one place and made it their job to know everything that was going on in their area. Other Travelers depended on them for news and tips on where to work or especially on places where the cops were buzzing. People sent them money every now and again to help them get by. Maybe Mom was calling one to see if she could find out anything about Jimmy and dealing and she didn't want me to know about it. But Berger, that was no Traveler name.

"Who do you think he could be?" I asked Ann later that night when we were giving each other manicures.

"I don't know," Ann said, holding out her hand for me.

She wanted a French manicure. I'd already done the coat of clear polish and was ready to start in on the white. I swirled the brush in the polish and then carefully traced the tip of her thumbnail. "All I keep thinking is it *must* have to do with Jimmy. What if he *is* dealing?"

Ann gasped. "Oh my God."

"What?"

Ann shook her head. "You're not gonna like this," she warned.

"What? Just tell me."

"You said there'd been other calls, right?"

"Yeah?"

Ann nodded knowingly. "Your mom's having an affair."

"Please!" I cried, slipping and smearing her whole next nail with polish. "This isn't one of your stupid books."

Ann pulled back her hand, dabbed a cotton ball with polish remover, and wiped off the messed-up nail. "Fine, don't believe me," she said with a huff.

Of course Ann wouldn't want to believe it could be about Jimmy. But Mom with anybody besides Dad? With a Country person? No way. "Where's she gonna meet a Country man?" I asked.

Ann shrugged. "People meet anywhere. Wal-Mart, for instance. The grocery store. The bank. Your mom goes to the bank."

"Not when we're on the road. Only when we're in Miami."

"Which explains why he's calling all of a sudden. They met in Miami, hit it off. . . ."

"But the area code wasn't Miami."

"He was there on vacation."

Ann had an answer for everything.

"Come on, think about it. Your dad's not exactly romantic."

I pictured Dad snoring in his recliner, empties by his feet. But just because Dad wasn't always giving her roses didn't mean Mom was having an affair. Ann held her hand out again for me to finish, but I didn't feel like it anymore.

"I don't think I can do the French part," I mumbled.

"Fine," Ann said, taking the bottle of polish from me.

When I walked home from Ann's, I heard Mom and Dad before I got within twenty feet of the trailer. They weren't fighting, but their voices were loud and charged.

"Jimmy's not going and that's that," Dad said. "You don't want him going to the *quad*—you said so yourself."

"No, I don't. But I don't want to lose him either. And this way we'll know what he's up to—we won't be wondering what he's gotten himself into."

Dad's tone softened. "You know how I feel about Jim. I have to draw the line here."

"You can't draw the line here," Mom pleaded. "Douglas, God, you know I don't want him to go either. But if we say no, that's it. He'll go anyway, and he won't come back. I can't do that again. . . . I won't."

"So what do you want me to do? Go with him? I go with him and I guarantee you Jim and I'll kill each other."

"What about Patrick? Patrick's at least got some common sense. Maybe he'll be smart enough to keep them both out of too much trouble. I wouldn't do this if I didn't already know how it'll turn out. You know just as well as—"

"Fine," Dad snapped, cutting her off. "I don't want to hear about it anymore. I'll go talk to the Murphys."

Dad burst out the door, and I pretended like I just happened to be walking up and hadn't heard anything. It didn't matter anyway because he strode past me like I wasn't even there. I opened the door to find Mom on the couch staring at nothing, her eyes watery.

"Bridget," she said. "I thought you were over at Ann's for the rest of the night."

I shrugged. "I got kind of sick of being there."

Mom brightened. "How about making cookies? Do you want to make cookies together?"

I cocked my head. "We haven't made cookies in forever."

"I know, and I was just thinking the other day that we

should." Mom stood up, opened the refrigerator door, and peered in. "We've got enough eggs and butter."

I smiled. There was no way Mom was having an affair. If she was having an affair with anything, it was her stove. Ann's crazy romance stories had definitely gone to her head. And there had to be a perfectly good explanation for the phone calls.

"Okay," I said. "If you want to."

It was good we made cookies because Dad gathered us all together for a barbecue the next day. Mom covered the card table with the red-checkered plastic tablecloth. Dad manned the grill, and soon the table was full of hot dogs and burgers, beer and chips, Mrs. Murphy's potato salad, and our chocolate-chunk cookies.

The first thing Ann said when she saw me was, "Any more calls?"

I shook my head. Even if there had been, I wouldn't have told her.

Mom and Dad and the Murphys and Big Jim mingled, eating, sloshing down beer, talking, even laughing at times, which I took to mean everything was all set for us to go to Arizona.

Patrick, Jimmy, Ann, and I ate away from the grown-ups, but I glanced over at Mom and Dad every once in a while. I thought I'd put Ann's crazy idea out of my head for good, but I found myself imagining what I'd think of Mom if I didn't know her. If she was pushing a shopping cart at Wal-Mart or in line at the bank. She was wearing slim white capri pants and a patterned sleeveless shirt, and she looked thirty, not forty. Lots of men would think she was pretty, and if one said something to her, flirted with her, well, maybe she *would* say something cute back. Then there was Dad in his faded and tattered work pants and shirt, the extra weight around his middle pushing over his belt. The more I looked at Mom next to Dad, the more I wondered if Ann could be right. And the more I couldn't stomach another bite of food.

As the last dogs and burgers were plucked off the table, Big Jim came over and clapped Patrick on the shoulder. "This is Bridget's man, I hear."

"Yes, sir," Patrick said proudly.

Big Jim shook his hand, gripping hard, and Patrick tried not to wince. "You're gonna take good care of my best girl, aren't you?" Big Jim asked him.

Patrick nodded.

"What's that?"

"Yes, sir," Patrick said.

Big Jim finally dropped his hand. "Good."

Before Mom brought out the ice cream and more beer, Dad whistled to get everybody's attention. "Okay, here are the ground rules."

Jimmy immediately smiled at Dad. Dad looked straight back at him while he spoke. "You listen to your uncle. You do exactly what he says."

"Of course," Jimmy said.

Big Jim glanced from Dad to Mr. Murphy. "I'll take good care of them. You know I will."

"You too, Bridget," Dad said, turning to me. "I'm counting on you."

I nodded. "Yes, Dad."

"When do we leave?" Jimmy asked.

"The day after next." Big Jim raised his beer. "To health, wealth, and family—and the time to enjoy them!"

After ice cream, Ann, Jimmy, Patrick, and I wandered off,

leaving Mom and Dad, Big Jim, and the Murphys to talk about the details. Like always, we just walked around the campground, going nowhere special.

"How awesome is this gonna be!" Jimmy practically yelled. "This is the big time. One hundred *kade*!" He and Patrick slapped hands.

Ann elbowed me. "You're so lucky you get to go."

I shrugged. "It's not that big a deal, really."

"Yes, it is. You guys are going practically across the country alone."

"We're not going alone—Big Jim'll be there."

"Yeah, but he doesn't care what you do."

"I'm not so sure about that. You don't know Big Jim."

When I thought about it, neither did any of us, really. He only popped into our lives every once in a while. But I got the feeling Big Jim believed more in the rules of our people than anyone thought he did, especially Dad.

"Still." Ann shrugged. "I'd go in your place in a second. It'll be totally cool."

"Ann's right," Patrick said. "It'll be awesome." He reached out for my hand. It was his way of asking if things were all right between us again. I wasn't sure if they were—all my emotions were still jumbled. But I gave him my hand anyway. He squeezed it once and then held it firmly, like he never wanted to let go again, and I realized Arizona *was* a big deal. It was weeks away from Mom and Dad. Weeks with only Jimmy and Big Jim and, more than anything, with Patrick. It would mean time to finally figure things out between us.

chapter 11

Mom tried not to cry when we left, but a few tears slipped out. We were standing just outside the trailer—Big Jim, Jimmy, Patrick, and me. She hugged Jimmy first and wouldn't let go.

"All right," Jimmy said, pulling away from her.

"We'll be back before you know it," I told her.

She stared at Jimmy. "You just be careful, okay?"

"Don't worry," Patrick said, looping his arm around my shoulders. "I'll take care of her."

But Mom wasn't worried about me. She smiled faintly at Patrick and then looked back at Jimmy.

Dad was in the trailer finishing his eggs. He wasn't even going to come out and say good-bye, but then Mom yelled to him, "They're leaving," and he stepped outside with half a piece of toast in his hand, still chewing.

Big Jim extended his hand to Dad. "Nothing to worry about, Douglas."

Dad stuffed the rest of the toast into his mouth and brushed the crumbs off on his work pants, then shook Big Jim's hand. "I'm counting on it."

Big Jim pumped his hand once more and turned to us. "Ready?"

"Shit, yeah," Jimmy said.

Patrick laughed. "I was born ready."

"Well, let's do it, then," Big Jim said, and headed for his truck.

Jimmy turned from Dad without so much as a good-bye, and Dad called after him, "Be careful now, you hear?"

Jimmy didn't answer and Dad looked at me. "We will be," I said.

We took both Big Jim's and Jimmy's trucks since four people cooped up in one truck for over twenty-two hundred miles wouldn't be pretty. Jimmy tossed Patrick his keys. "You want to start out? I'll ride with Big Jim."

"Sure," Patrick said. Then he looked at me. "Let's go, babe-alicious."

"Babe-alicious?" I laughed.

Patrick shrugged. "I don't know where that came from."

Patrick and I hopped into Jimmy's truck, and Jimmy jogged to catch up to Big Jim. Patrick started the engine and I rolled down my window, then we followed Big Jim and Jimmy out of the campground entrance. I stuck my head out the window and looked back at Mom and Dad. Jimmy must have rolled down his window too because I heard him scream, "Woo-hoo!" Mom waved, but Dad headed back inside the trailer. I watched Mom, her hand raised high in the air, still waving at us, until we turned the corner.

As we pulled onto the highway, Patrick reached out and squeezed my thigh. "We're off." He tuned the radio to a classic rock station that was playing "Sweet Home Alabama." He turned it up loud and started singing. "Come on, Bridge," he said.

I joined in and we both belted out the words. Patrick thumped the steering wheel and I bobbed in my seat. We were leaving the South and everything we knew, headed for a part of the country we'd never seen. Patrick and Jimmy had to feel it too, the rush of not knowing what waited for us out there. Maybe this was what Jimmy always felt when he did big jobs. Maybe this was why it thrilled him so. What we usually did—Kmarts, driveways—had its danger, but for the most part it was routine. It stirred me to not know what was coming next.

When the song ended and a commercial came on, Patrick turned the radio down and I asked him if his parents were sad to see him go. He shrugged. "Not really."

"My parents couldn't have cared less about me," I said with a huff. "They only care about Jimmy."

"That's not true," Patrick said. "They care about you. They just trust you more, that's all."

I looked out the window as we passed a sagging farmhouse with peeling paint. "I'm not so sure I want to be trusted."

"What are you talking about?"

"I'm talking about not always doing the right thing—the thing you're supposed to do. Don't you ever want to do the wrong thing?"

Patrick rolled his eyes. "Is the whole trip gonna be like this?"

"Like what?"

"Like all these questions. Do you always have to think everything through so much?"

I turned back to Patrick. He kept his eyes on the road, but I could tell he felt my stare. "Don't you want to know me?" I asked. If this was ever going to work between us, I knew it'd have to be different than other Traveler marriages. Different than Mom and Dad's marriage. I needed us to be best friends—I couldn't settle for less. We'd have to know each other, really know each other, or we wouldn't be able to love each other.

He glanced at me. "Of course I want to know you."

"Well, this is me."

With his eyes back on the road, Patrick said, "I know. I love that about you—how you're always reading and thinking about things. You're so smart. It's just that . . ." Patrick paused and then began again. "It's just that I don't think like that. I don't think about all the things you do. And I worry that's gonna matter to you."

"It doesn't matter," I blurted out, though I wasn't sure if I meant it. But instead of thinking about whether I did mean it or *could* mean it, I thought about what Patrick had just said about loving me. It wasn't *I love you,* but it was the closest we'd ever come. I scooted over closer to him and he threw his arm around me. The commercial ended and an Eagles song came on, and we both started singing again.

We drove sixteen hours straight, only stopping for bathroom, gas, and food breaks. Big Jim wanted to make it over the Texas border by the end of the day. That would leave the rest of Texas, all of New Mexico, and part of Arizona for the day after.

Traveling in Jimmy's truck was different. As far as putting on real mileage, going hundreds, thousands, of miles, I'd only done that in the back of a trailer. A trailer's ride was smooth, skimming over the pavement. In a truck, each spin of the tires jolted you in your seat; each crack in the blacktop bit into your back.

Just past Fayetteville I fell asleep, a hard sleep filled with dreams that I couldn't quite remember, which I was glad for. Every night since Belle Springs, Jared had worked his way into my dreams. He wasn't always beaten and bloody. Sometimes it was before Jimmy found us. Once I was supposed to marry Jared instead of Patrick. I wasn't sure what that dream meant, but it left me feeling empty all day.

The neon light from the OPEN 24 HOURS sign at the truck stop woke me. Patrick leaned over the seat to where I was curled up with his jacket against the window. He said in a soft voice, "You need to go?"

I sat up and yawned. "Yeah."

Inside the truck stop Patrick stood in line for sodas while I went to the bathroom. When I came out he was still in line, so I roamed the gift shop looking at bumper stickers and T-shirts that said DON'T MESS WITH TEXAS. I thought about sending Ann a postcard with a huge angry bull on it that said LOOKING FOR BEEFCAKE? But by the time it reached the campground in Greensboro, they'd have moved on. Patrick came in while I was choosing a pack of gum and handed me my soda. I settled on Juicy Fruit and was heading to the counter when I spotted one of those throwaway cameras on the sale rack.

I held it up to Patrick. "Let's get it. We can take pictures and bring them back to show Ann and everybody."

I wasn't sure who "everybody" was, but the idea of taking pictures sounded like so much fun. We'd never had a camera growing up, and except for one of those snapshots Ann and I got once at a county fair, I couldn't ever remember someone taking my picture. Given our life, the kind of evidence photos provided wasn't a good thing to have around. I thought about other families and how they were always snapping photos. How they had stacks of albums accounting for their lives. How we had nothing to show for where we'd been, what we'd done, who we were.

"I don't know, Bridget," Patrick said. I tried my most pleading look and he caved. "Okay, fine, but get it and let's go. The Jims are waiting outside."

When we got back to the truck, Jimmy was sitting on the front bumper.

"Big Jim kick you out?" Patrick asked.

"He says he's just used to being alone."

Patrick chuckled. "He kicked you out."

"He just needs some time alone. That's all."

"Sure," Patrick said, still smiling.

Jimmy took over driving. We were quiet for a while, Patrick and me sucking down our sodas. Jimmy broke the silence, talking about Big Jim. "He scores big, and I mean *big*."

"Yeah?" Patrick said.

Jimmy's voice was excited and intense. "He told me about this one time he convinced this trucker hauling TVs to department stores to go door-to-door with him instead. They said they were last year's models. He's always pulling jobs like that. Those are the kind of jobs we should be doing."

"What do you think we're doing right now?" Patrick asked.

"But I mean *only* doing big jobs, no more paving driveways. Or even selling trees like I did. I thought that was so big-time. Now I see what's really big-time. You know what I mean?"

"I guess," Patrick said.

"No, you don't," Jimmy scoffed. "I know you—you're more like my father. Happy just scraping by."

Patrick came right back at him, his tone testy. "I'm here right now, aren't I?"

"Yeah," Jimmy said. "But it's different."

"How?"

"This is a one time deal for you. For me, it's gonna be a way of life."

Jimmy reached down and turned up the radio. He stared out at the road intently as he drove, not even listening to the station he'd turned on, like if he concentrated on the road hard enough, he'd be free of Dad forever.

I spoke up so Jimmy could hear me over the blaring music. "But wouldn't it be lonely?"

"Hell no," Jimmy said. "You think Big Jim's lonely? He just kicked me out of his truck because he was sick of *not* being alone."

"It's what you really want?" I asked. "To have no one but yourself to worry about?"

"Yeah," he said flatly. "It is."

I envied him that. I envied him knowing what he really wanted.

At the motel, I locked the bathroom door and ran a bath. Jimmy and I shared one room and Patrick and Big Jim had the next room over. Growing up in trailers, I could count the times I'd taken a bath on one hand. I shivered in anticipation as water filled the tub, and when I couldn't wait anymore I climbed in. I sat in the few inches of water as more poured in, cupped my hands, and splashed my face over and over again with the steaming water.

When the tub was full, I turned off the faucet and eased back, letting the water cover me. The world quieted; my body stilled. Even in a parked trailer, somehow I never felt rooted. I always felt like I was in motion. In the bath, though, I felt like

I was actually somewhere, and I wanted that feeling to last as long as it could.

After a while the water cooled. I let some out, refilled the tub with hot water, and lay back for another long while. I didn't think of Patrick or Mom or the job but just felt the calming water . . . that is, until Jimmy pounded on the door.

"What the hell are you doing in there?" he shouted. "You've been in there over an hour."

I was sure Country girls spent as much time as they wanted in the bathroom. "I'm taking a bath," I yelled back. "And don't tell me I'm using up all the hot water because we're in a hotel."

"It's a *mo*tel," Jimmy said.

It was a motel—and not a particularly nice one either. There were ugly brown curtains and matching brown comforters on the beds. But it was still more space in one room than I'd ever had before.

When I finally did get out, I wanted to wrap one towel around my body and one around my head like girls did on TV shows. But there were only two thin towels, and Jimmy would have been pissed if I used his, so I dried off with the one, put on my pajamas, and then wrapped the damp towel around my head.

Jimmy was watching some old Western on TV, and as I sat down on my bed I asked him if we could watch something else.

"You should call Mom, tell her we got in okay," he said.

"You call her. She only cares about you."

"She only *worries* about me," Jimmy pointed out. "There's a difference."

Even though I knew Mom also definitely *cared* about Jimmy, I was surprised that Jimmy knew how Mom worried over him. I'd always thought he'd only seen it from his side— the side of feeling hassled.

"Well, if you'd just agree to settle down, maybe—"

Jimmy cut me off. "Don't you start too."

"But if you marry Ann, Mom and Dad'll lay off and you can do whatever you want—go off and do the big jobs. Mr. Murphy wouldn't care about you sticking around as long as you brought in enough money."

"He'd care about me leaving his daughter home for months at a time." Jimmy shook his head. "Don't you see? If I agree to marry her, it's even more reason I can't be out risking things."

For the first time I did see. For Jimmy too the *M* word meant changes you had to be ready to accept.

"So it's not Ann?" I asked. I wanted to know so if the time came I could comfort Ann with that at least.

"No," Jimmy sighed. "It's not Ann. Ann's fine. I mean, she's pretty and she's nice and all."

"Then why do you always act like she's got *cooties* or something?"

"Because I'm not gonna lead her on. I'm not gonna let her think there's a chance when there just isn't."

I'd always thought Jimmy was just being mean to Ann, but now I saw how he was really looking out for her. It would've been easy for him to mess around with Ann a little, or even a lot, since she was so into him. It wasn't because he didn't like her but because maybe he did, and he didn't want to give himself any room to make a mistake that would hurt her more than it would him.

"Well, I'm not so sure I want to marry Patrick either," I said.

"You're stupid if you don't," Jimmy warned. "Patrick's awesome." I knew Jimmy meant it more than just the way a person thinks his best friend is awesome. "Patrick's a better man than me, that's for sure," Jimmy added. "A better man than most. Shit, you know that."

"Maybe it isn't Patrick. Like how with you it isn't Ann."

Jimmy shook his head. "It's different."

I wanted to ask him why it was different, even though I was pretty sure I knew. It had to do with a Traveler woman needing a man and a Traveler man not needing a woman. I didn't get to ask, anyway, because Jimmy said, "Speaking of all this marriage stuff, I wasn't even going to say anything, it's so wrong, but just so you know, Mom's not having an affair."

"Ann told you?" I hadn't sworn her to secrecy. I hadn't thought I'd needed to, but I should've known better. When it came to Jimmy, Ann couldn't keep her mouth shut.

"Did she tell you about the weird phone calls? About Russell Berger?" I at least wanted to make sure she'd given Jimmy all the facts.

Jimmy nodded.

"Well? How do you explain all that?"

Jimmy's voice was stern. "Listen, I'm telling you. She's *not* having an affair with Russell Berger."

"But how do you know?"

Jimmy stared at me. "I just know. Now I don't want to hear anything else about it." I bit my lip. Maybe it was his stern tone, or maybe it was that I really didn't want to know what the call was about, or maybe it was because he'd saved me back in Belle Springs and I'd owe him forever for that, but I didn't press Jimmy further and I called Mom.

She answered her cell after half a ring. "I've been waiting all day for a call from you guys. How's Jimmy?"

"He's right here if you want to talk to him."

Jimmy wagged his head no. He grabbed his lighter and pack of cigarettes off the dresser and headed outside.

"He's fine," I added. "But he's going next door to talk to Big Jim."

As the door clicked shut behind Jimmy, Mom asked, "So how's Patrick?"

"I'm great, Mom, thanks for asking," I said.

"Come on, Bridget." Mom paused but still didn't ask how I was. "So things are better between you two?"

"I guess," I mumbled. Even after what Jimmy had said about Patrick being so great, and even though things *were* better now, it didn't mean I was ready. And I had to know. "Mom?" I asked. "Is the date really set?"

"I'm not gonna lie to you."

I swallowed hard. My stomach felt like a hazmat truck had crashed inside it, spilling toxic acids.

"I know it's scary," she said.

"No, you don't," I snapped back.

"Yes, I do. I didn't know your father half as well as you know Patrick."

"But it's not just marrying him."

"Then what is it?" Mom asked.

I held my breath and thought about telling Mom. I needed someone who'd understand in a way Jimmy couldn't because he was a man. But would Mom understand? Before I could make up my mind, her call-waiting beeped. She clicked over, and when she came back a few seconds later she said, "It's important. I have to take it."

"Let me guess, business?" I said sarcastically.

Mom breathed a sigh but didn't respond.

"Where's Dad?" I asked. "Doesn't he want to talk to Jimmy?"

"He's out," Mom said. "I gotta go, honey."

Another call, conveniently when Dad was out. Maybe Ann was right and Mom was having an affair. But Jimmy's voice was so stern and the way he'd said, *"She's not having an affair with Russell Berger,"* it was like he knew Russell Berger. Otherwise he would've just said, *She's not having an affair.* So maybe I was right and it was about Jimmy. One thing I hadn't done was find out where the area code was from. I wasn't sure what it would tell me, but it was at least another piece of information. I called 411 and asked what state the 617 area code was in.

Massachusetts. Boston.

Mom didn't know anyone in Boston, as far as I knew. Boston. I lay back on the bed and racked my brain for anything I'd ever heard Mom or anybody else mention about Boston.

It was a few minutes before I heard Jared's voice in my head. *"I'm down here from up north."*

chapter 12

I'll never forget seeing my first real live cactus. I'd seen small ones in stores and some on TV, but it was strange to see real ones—five, even six feet tall, rooted in the dry and cracked earth on the side of the road, their arms outstretched. I guess it'd be like seeing a palm tree for the first time if you'd never been to Florida. I thought it was so cool, I made Patrick pull over and snap a picture of me standing next to one.

In Florence we checked into the Florence Good-Nightingale Motel. I asked Big Jim if we'd be staying there the whole time because it was always nice to stay in one place for more than a few days. He said we'd see how it went—we might have to move around or drive from farther away if people started noticing us.

The next morning Big Jim woke us early, banging on the door that connected Jimmy's and my room to his and Patrick's. "Let's go! We gotta have a look at what we're gonna be selling."

What we were selling were condos—and of course we weren't selling them legit. The contractor who built them had messed up and they weren't up to code. But instead of putting the money into fixing them, he'd called a guy he knew would find him a Realtor who wouldn't ask questions. That guy knew Big Jim, and he cut a deal that for ten percent of the money the scam was Big Jim's.

The condos were a few miles from the motel, stucco units strung together so that they looked like one huge house, only each unit had its own door and its own garage. Big Jim, Jimmy, and Patrick got out of the truck to go inside, but I stayed back. Jimmy didn't notice, just headed for the entrance to the first unit. It was Patrick who came over to the truck and looked in.

"You're not coming?"

I shook my head.

"How come?"

"Just don't feel like it."

I waited in the truck while they checked out the units and made sure they were clean and in good order. I didn't want to see inside—the kitchen sink, the bathtub, the closet in the bedroom. If I did, I'd just picture people's stuff in there. A small plant by the sink, shampoo bottles on the rim of the bathtub, running sneakers in the closet. Then I'd think about how the people wouldn't actually be buying the condos—how they'd put down their money and we'd take it and run, leaving them and the contractor high and dry. Maybe I was going soft, but I didn't care. Patrick could fill me in on the details I'd need to know to do my job, but I didn't want any mental pictures.

"They're nice," Patrick said when they came back out. "They'll be easy to sell."

Next we drove to what was going to be our office, which was only a few miles from the condos. It was in a little cluster of recently built stores—a copy place, a Mexican restaurant, and a carpet store—just outside of the strip of road that was "town." The office had been a pack-and-ship place before the copy center started offering the same services. They'd left a large counter, two desks, one broken lamp, and a few plastic trash cans.

Inside it was hot and stale, so we turned the AC on and propped the door open to get some fresh air. Arizona was hotter in pure temperature than many of the Southern states, but it wasn't as humid, and the dry air from outside felt good.

Big Jim motioned to one of the desks. "Give me a hand here, boys. We're gonna move this one up to the front by the window." Big Jim looked at me. "This'll be Bridget's desk."

Jimmy and Patrick picked up the desk and Big Jim showed them where to put it. Then they moved the other desk to the small office at the back, which would be Big Jim's. Big Jim strode back to the middle of the store and rested a hand on the huge counter. "Now what in the hell are we gonna do with this thing?"

The counter was chest-high and white. I pictured people leaning on it while waiting to place their orders—sending a care package to their daughter at sleepaway camp, sending a birthday present to a great-aunt who lived all alone in a concrete apartment building, sending back a mail-order purchase. Then all of a sudden I pictured chairs around the counter, really high chairs, and people sitting in them. "I have an idea."

"Shoot," Big Jim said.

"What if it was like a big conference-room table or something? We could get chairs—you know, high ones with backs? Then when people come in and you guys meet with them, you could sit around it."

"Like in a big law firm on TV or something," Patrick joined in.

"Yeah," I said. "Exactly."

Big Jim nodded. "I like it. Good idea, Bridget."

I tried to keep from smiling. When had Mom or Dad ever said to me, *"Good idea"*? When had anybody? "All we need are the chairs," I added.

We got the chairs and everything else we needed that afternoon at a Wal-Mart a few towns over so nobody would see us. Because this was a big job with a big take, we bought the stuff proper. For a hundred *kade,* we wouldn't nickel-and-dime.

Not stealing meant I didn't need to case the aisles or check for workers who looked like they gave a shit about their job. I didn't need to look at whatever it was we wanted and figure out how I could slip it into my bag or under my coat. We plucked things off the shelves and held them where anyone could see them, walked to the checkout, and laid them down on the counter.

We bought two phones—one with all sorts of HOLD buttons on it for me so it'd look serious and one with a fax machine— four chairs for the big table, a chair for me and a chair for Big Jim, a few lamps, some of those pink WHILE YOU WERE OUT notepads, pens, a coffeemaker, coffee, filters, and cups.

After we'd taken all the stuff back and set it up, I sat at my desk with my lamp and phone and pink notepad and pens, and a chill of excitement ran through me. It was going to be fun to work for real again.

When we got back to the motel, Patrick knocked on our door. He said he was planning to call Ann and knew she'd want to talk to me. I wondered if maybe calling Ann was just an excuse for him to come over. If it was, it was kind of cute. With our parents arranging our marriage, Patrick and I'd never had the chance for any of the stuff I saw kids doing in school—passing notes, asking friends to find out who liked who, instant-messaging or paging each other. Patrick coming over was like a boy just showing up at a girl's house with some lame excuse why he's there, to get a homework assignment or something, when really he just wants to see her.

"I'm not here," Jimmy said when Patrick picked up the phone and started dialing. "I'm hitting the shower."

Patrick rolled his eyes. It was all he would do when Jimmy was a shit about Ann—he never called him on it. I guess because he understood better than I had that Jimmy wasn't ever going to marry her and that his being annoyed by her was much better than giving her false hope.

As I listened to Patrick fill Ann in on the trip, I hoped maybe she wouldn't ask for Jimmy after all. But then Patrick said, "No, but Bridget's right here," and I knew she had. Poor Ann. When would she give up? When would she stop thinking this was one of her romance stories where if the girl hangs in there long enough the guy comes around to loving her?

Patrick handed me the phone. The first thing Ann said when I got on was, "How is he?"

"You just talked to him. He's fine," I answered, knowing she didn't mean Patrick.

"Come on, Bridget. I miss him. Do you think he misses me, even in the slightest?"

Maybe I should've been as harsh as Jimmy was at times. Maybe then I'd've been a better friend. But it just seemed too cruel. So instead I mumbled, "All he's thinking about is the job."

There was a moment's silence. Then Ann spoke again. "So how *is* Patrick?"

I looked over where Patrick was now lying on Jimmy's bed, watching the day's baseball highlights on ESPN.

"Come on," Ann prodded.

"He's fine."

"You still a virgin?" Her tone was teasing, but I knew she was also wondering.

"I'm not answering that," I teased her back.

"Well, you'll be glad to know, I've been keeping tabs on your mom for you."

"And?"

"I heard her on the phone talking about decorating a house—you know, curtains and carpeting and stuff."

"A house?" The only people we knew who had houses lived in Murphy Village.

"It was a house. They were talking about the measurements—ten by sixteen for one room. This wasn't any trailer. Maybe your mom's planning to leave your dad. Maybe her and Russell Berger are buying a new house together."

"I'm sure there's some other explanation." It did seem weird, but after what Jimmy had said and finding out Russell Berger's area code, I was pretty sure it was about Jared. But I couldn't tell Ann that because of Patrick. I hadn't told her anything about Jared or that night.

"Maybe," Ann said, but I could tell she didn't really think so. "What do you think would happen—you know, if your dad found out?"

"I don't know," I grumbled. I was getting sick of Ann's crazy imagination.

"Remember the Donahues?"

"No."

"He killed her when he found out she was sleeping with the

121

owner of the campground they were staying at. Shot her right between the eyes at close range. They couldn't even be sure it was her at first. He blew her whole face off."

Even though I didn't believe Mom was having an affair, suddenly I felt shaky. Maybe because if it was really about Jared, it would be worse. What if he or his family was black-mailing us or coming to get revenge? "I gotta go," I said.

"I didn't mean that your—"

"It's okay." I cut her off. "I just gotta go."

When I hung up, Patrick asked, "Who's got a house?"

"Ann just saw one she liked," I mumbled.

Patrick looked from the TV to me. "Has that girl lost her mind?"

"Yes," I said. "She has."

chapter 13

Flynn Realty. How may I direct your call?"

Big Jim placed an ad in the newspaper, and the calls rolled in. Flynn was the name we used. Big Jim was Jim Flynn. Jimmy was his son and I was his daughter. Patrick was our cousin. A regular good old family business.

I'd give the caller the basic information about the condos. How many units, how many rooms, how much. Right from the beginning if someone asked how many units were left, I'd say only seventeen. Next I'd invite the caller to come in for an appointment. Whatever day they wanted to come in, though, I'd say we were booked up. But then I'd hesitate, and I'd spout excitedly, *"Wait a second, I made a mistake. I just realized we have a cancellation and we can fit you in after all!"*

If the person asked to talk to a Realtor, I'd put them on hold. After thirty seconds or so I'd come back on and tell them all our Realtors were with other customers, but I could have one call them back. All this was to build up people's interest. Big Jim said people always wanted what other people wanted. But he always made sure to call them back within a half hour because he also said people liked to be treated as if they were important.

Big Jim coached Jimmy and Patrick on what to say and how to act with customers. He even made them practice. He pretended to be a customer and came up with different questions and comments each time.

Before our first appointment, Big Jim sat us down at the conference table for a pep talk.

"Okay," he began, "I think all three of you already know that this is a big job. Some of our people go their whole lives and never pull off something like this. Never."

As Big Jim talked, I thought of Dad filling up the tanks on the truck day after day. Did Dad ever dream of this type of scam? What was it that made him and Big Jim so different? And him and Jimmy, for that matter? And who was smarter? Dad, who stuck to safe jobs that brought just enough money to get by, or Big Jim, who risked everything for the big payoff?

"I didn't pull a job like this until I was much older than y'all," Big Jim continued. "Of course, I didn't have anyone to teach me, which gets me to the next thing I have to say. This is your chance if you want it. Yes, I *need* you to act right. To come home with the money and to come home period, we have to make them believe we're legit. But you can also learn a lot if you want to."

Jimmy stared at Big Jim like he was trying to memorize every word coming out of his mouth. Patrick nodded along, but he didn't look as into it.

"You got a question about anything, you ask me," Big Jim warned. "Don't go messing up because you're too proud to admit you don't know. That's what gets people in trouble—acting out of pride instead of smarts. You got it?"

"Yes," Jimmy said.

Big Jim looked at Patrick and then at me. "That goes for both of you too. And another thing: Don't forget where you're from and who you are. Even when those checks come rolling in—and believe me, they will—don't go getting cocky because that's when you trip up. I don't want to see you trip up at all, but I sure as hell don't want you tripping up on my time and costing me anything—losing money or, worse, getting us caught."

I guess Big Jim decided he'd scared us enough because he stood up and announced, "All right, let's go. There's someone we gotta talk to before we get this thing started."

"Who?" Jimmy asked.

"God," Big Jim replied. "If you want a job to go well, you gotta pray to the big guy."

Mom dragged us to church whenever she could during the winter and even sometimes when we were on the road. Even though most Travelers had First Communion, not all kept going to church. Like so many other things in our culture, it'd slipped away from generation to generation, and I was surprised to find that of all Travelers Big Jim was religious. But we piled into Big Jim's truck anyway, me sitting on Patrick's lap with Jimmy wedged between us and Big Jim.

Big Jim pulled over to the curb next to two women in spandex shorts pushing big-wheeled baby joggers. He told Patrick to roll down his window. Big Jim leaned in front of us and called to the women, "Excuse me, where's the nearest house of worship around here?"

They definitely must have thought it was weird, the four of us piled into the pickup, enormous Big Jim leaning out the window and asking where to find the closest church. But one of the women answered politely, "Back up the road about a half mile. You can turn around at the next light."

Big Jim thanked her, but instead of going down to the next light, he whipped a U-turn. A car zoomed from the other direction and Big Jim stepped on the gas, the wheels of the truck squealing.

We went back the half mile and pulled up to a small one-story cement building. The sign out front read FIRST CHURCH OF FLORENCE. We parked in the lot, which only had one other car in it. It didn't look anything like St. Peter's, the huge stone church we went to in Miami.

As we followed Big Jim to the church door, Jimmy whispered the obvious to Patrick and me. "This ain't a Catholic church."

Big Jim heard him and cautioned, "There's only one God, Jimmy. Always remember that."

Inside, the church was completely different too. It was plain, simple—no stained-glass windows, no statues of Mary, no holy water, no bank of candles, no confessionals. I couldn't even find a crucifix. There was a cross above the altar, but it was bare, no Jesus on it. The church was empty except for a woman mopping the tile floor. We walked toward her down the aisle. She looked up at us and stopped mopping.

"Excuse me, when's your next mass?" Big Jim asked politely.

"Our next *service* is tomorrow at ten," she said, eyeing us warily.

"We'll just pray, then."

The woman nodded and stepped aside to let us by. We followed Big Jim into one of the pews at the front of the church. Big Jim knelt and crossed himself like we always did before entering the pew. Jimmy and Patrick followed, and I looked back at the woman, who hadn't resumed her mopping. She stared at us like what we were doing was strange. I quickly knelt and crossed myself and slid into the pew next to Patrick.

I searched the floor in front of me. There were no kneelers like at St. Peter's, but that didn't look like it fazed Big Jim. He knelt right on the tile floor and closed his eyes. It was odd to see him praying, his huge body folded over, his knees grinding into the hard floor. Big Jim seemed to have his own loose definition of religion. But he still had one, that was for sure.

The tile floor was surprisingly cold even through my pants. I wondered if Big Jim was just praying for the job to go smoothly or if there were other things he prayed for. It seemed funny to pray to God to put one over on people.

I looked at him kneeling there, his eyes closed. A large scar ran from his temple to his chin on the right side of his face. When I was really young, I was scared of it, and scared of him too. I'd hide behind Mom anytime he'd show up. But then one time he took me on his lap and let me touch it, run my fingers all over it, and it didn't feel much different than regular skin. He told me someone had knifed him in a fight long before I was born.

I wondered if maybe Big Jim prayed for things to be better between him and Dad or maybe he prayed for his ex-wife. I tried to pray, but mostly I just thought about Mom and Jimmy and Russell Berger. If Jimmy knew for sure Mom wasn't having an affair, why didn't he tell me how he knew? The fact that he didn't give me reasons made me think he knew and was hiding something awful about Jared. But then there was what Ann had said about the house. Maybe Jimmy knew Mom was leaving Dad to marry a Country man and buy a house and he was trying to stop her and just didn't want me to worry.

I caught myself. My imagination was getting worse than Ann's. I took a deep breath and prayed that none of it was true. I prayed that there was some perfectly good explanation for the calls that had nothing to do with an affair or Jared or Jimmy dealing. I apologized for not being in the right church and I hoped that, like Big Jim said, God would understand.

chapter 14

Our first appointment was for one Mr. Richard Ruby.

Twenty minutes before he was due in I went to the bathroom to check how I looked. I was wearing a long skirt with a matching sweater set. It was one of the outfits we'd bought when Mom and Mrs. Murphy took Jimmy, Patrick, and me shopping for professional-looking clothes the day before we left. I'd twisted my hair back into a bun, and the eyeliner and lipstick I'd put on so I'd look older were still fresh. I liked the way I looked. I could be working anywhere, in a bank, in a law office, in a fancy department store.

Patrick and Jimmy were dressed up too. Both were clean-shaven and wore pressed pants that the woman at the clothing store had called slacks. Both also had on starched button-down shirts and polished dress shoes. It was funny to see Patrick out of his usual grease-stained pants and T-shirt. For a second I wondered what he'd do for a living if he wasn't a Traveler.

Mr. Ruby's voice was soft on the phone, so I was surprised to see a short, stout man with a gray buzz cut come through the door. He walked with a slight hitch and wore a faded leather jacket.

"Hello," I greeted him. "Can I help you?"

"Richard Ruby, I have an appointment."

I scanned the day planner on my desk and stopped my finger at his name, written in among a handful of fake names so it'd look like we were chock-full. "Here you are. Let me get Jim for you."

Big Jim was in the back with Jimmy and Patrick. "Tell him I'll be out in a second and give him a listing sheet," he told me.

Back outside, I showed Mr. Ruby to the conference table and asked if I could get him some coffee. "It's hazelnut," I added.

"Why not," he said. "I don't usually have coffee in the afternoon, but why not."

I brought over a listing sheet with the coffee. We'd picked up a few from other realty places and copied their lingo. Ours read: *Charming and comfortable newly built condo units in desirable Taber Hill area. One- and two-bedrooms available. Each unit has its own one-car garage. Walk to town, park, and Middleton School. These homes await your personal touch.*

Mr. Ruby glanced over the listing sheet, then put it down and looked back at me. "Let me guess, you're working here to put yourself through school. You go to State?"

I smiled and shook my head. "Actually Jim's my father. I help out. It's a family business—everyone pitches in."

"But you're in school, right?"

"Well, it's summer now," I said.

"But when it's not summer?"

I fell easily into the lie. "Yes. I do go to State."

"What are you studying?"

130

I thought of my paper on the Black Sox that I'd left behind in Miami. "History."

"American? European?"

"American."

"You study any of the wars yet?" Mr. Ruby asked. "Wartime is when history is made."

"How do you mean?"

"War pushes people to make decisions that might not otherwise get made. History-altering decisions."

"You seem to know a lot about war," I said.

Mr. Ruby straightened. "Retired colonel, U.S. Army."

"So you fought in wars?"

"Vietnam. Talk about decisions being made. Or not made, as it were."

I wanted to hear more. I could've talked to Mr. Ruby and pretended I was a student at State all day—I hardly ever talked to Country folk. But I didn't get to because Big Jim, Jimmy, and Patrick came out from the back office. Big Jim shook Mr. Ruby's hand. "Jim Flynn," he said.

Even though he was a good foot shorter than Big Jim, Mr. Ruby didn't look small next to him. As they talked, I went back to my desk and pretended to file some papers so I could listen in.

"How long have you been at this location?" Mr. Ruby asked.

"Well, we've been in business twenty years, but we've only been here a couple of weeks," Big Jim explained. "What we are is contractual Realtors. We work for the companies that build the developments. They hire us to travel, mostly regionally, set up the offices, and help match the right people with the new developments, whether those be condos, houses, or apartments."

"I see," Mr. Ruby said.

"We're a family-run business. It was my brother and me before these kids were even born. He's got diabetes, though, and the driving back and forth to show places got to be too much for him. Now tell me. Just what are you looking for in a home?"

Mr. Ruby explained that he lived alone and wanted a clean, small, livable place. "I don't have the time or energy for dealing with the lawn and upkeep of a house. These condos sounded like they might be a good alternative."

"They are indeed," Big Jim said. "You know what, I'm not gonna go through it all, give you the big song and dance about why they might be perfect for you. I can see you know what you want, plain and simple. Let's just head on out and have a look."

Mr. Ruby nodded. "Sounds good."

Big Jim knew how to play people—even people like Mr. Ruby, who you could tell wouldn't stand for much BS. It was easier with a pigeon drop or a driveway job, where you picked out just the right person. With this you couldn't control who might walk through that door. You had to work on the fly.

Big Jim told Jimmy and Patrick to pull the truck around from the parking lot out back, and they headed out the door.

After they'd left, Mr. Ruby said to Big Jim, "I hope you don't mind me asking, but that's some scar you got there."

I held my breath, wondering if I was wrong and Mr. Ruby saw right through everything. But Big Jim was smooth. "Don't mind at all. Did a bit of logging growing up. Got slashed pretty good by a branch."

Big Jim paused at my desk on his way out the door with Mr. Ruby. "Now, my girl here," he said, looking at me. "She's my pride and joy."

"I can see why," Mr. Ruby said. "She seems like a smart one, studying at State and all."

My stomach dropped, but Big Jim didn't miss a beat.

"Oh yes," he added. "She's very smart, all right."

Jimmy and Patrick pulled the truck up in front of the office, and I started breathing again. There was nothing to worry about. Big Jim was skilled. The magnetic sign he'd had made was on the truck door. The sign was so good it looked like the lettering was written straight on the truck. FLYNN REALTY, A FAMILY BUSINESS FOR OVER 20 YEARS.

Pretty soon Jimmy and Patrick took people out to the units on their own. Everything was going smoothly, and when I was setting up appointments or handing out listing sheets, I forgot about the scam. I caught myself picturing people moving into the condos and us bringing by a nice plant with a note: *Welcome to your new home, from all of us at Flynn Realty.*

On Friday, a week and a half after we'd gotten there, our first deposit came in. The couple signed a fake purchase and sale agreement and handed over the check for five thousand dollars made out to Flynn Realty. The next day Big Jim would deposit it in the bank account he'd opened a few towns over. The account was in the name of Jim Flynn—it turned out Big Jim had a fake Arizona driver's license and everything all made up for Jim Flynn. And the minute that check cleared, Big Jim would take the money back out. We'd stay as long as we could and deposit as many checks as possible. When someone asked too many questions or the contractor called about his money, we'd take off with whatever we'd made, which Big Jim figured would be at least a hundred grand. And the contractor probably wouldn't come after us because he'd been trying to sell the units even though they weren't up to code.

That night Big Jim took us to the Starving Steer Steak House to celebrate the deposit. The sign above the restaurant had a cartoon cow salivating over a piece of steak, which was pretty stupid when you thought about it because cows don't eat meat and even if they did, they certainly wouldn't eat their own kind. It was dark inside, and my eyes had to adjust. We sat in a huge round booth, which didn't look as big once Big Jim had his arms over the sides of it.

Big Jim didn't even look at a menu. When the waitress came he ordered top sirloin for all of us. When I told him I didn't want it, he thumped a hand down on the table. "We're having a little celebration here. You gotta eat up."

"I'd just rather have the chicken," I told him. Something about that sign had made me lose my taste for steak.

Big Jim leaned back in the booth. "Fine, so long as you eat. I can't be bringing you back all skinny 'cause I didn't feed you right. Your mother'll kill me."

"Mom, kill you?" Jimmy snickered. "That's a laugh."

Big Jim turned serious. "Your mother's a tough woman. Don't you get that wrong."

"Why's she so tough?" I asked. Worrying about Jimmy and buckling to whatever Dad said didn't seem particularly tough. But maybe Big Jim knew things about Mom I didn't know. If Russell Berger was calling about Jimmy and Jared and Mom was handling it on her own and keeping it from Dad, then she really was pretty tough.

"She's been through a lot," Big Jim said. "A lot y'all can never imagine."

"Like what?"

"Like nothing young girls should worry over."

"Come on," I pleaded. "What's there about Mom you can't tell us?"

Big Jim looked at me sternly, and his "That's enough, Bridget" quieted me.

For all his roughness with others, Big Jim had never spoken harshly to me, and his words scalded. I looked away, and he must've known he'd hurt me because he grabbed his napkin from the table, tucked it into his shirt collar just below his chin, and said, "Where's our food now? I'm so hungry my stomach thinks my throat's been slit! Aren't you hungry, honey?"

"Sure," I mumbled.

When we climbed into the truck to head home, Big Jim asked Jimmy and Patrick if they wanted to go out. Both of them said yes. I knew Patrick had to say yes, but I'd still hoped he wouldn't. That somehow Arizona would be different. That spending more time with me would make him different.

Big Jim swung into the motel parking lot right up to the door of the room I shared with Jimmy. I stepped down from the truck and he rolled down his window and called after me, "You okay?"

"Fine," I muttered.

As they pulled out, I reached in my purse for the throwaway camera. Since posing next to the cactus I'd taken one picture of Patrick in the ten-gallon hat he'd gotten in Texas and one of Jimmy in bed in the morning when he had puffy eyes and bad bed-head. I thought that might be a good one to show Ann. Patrick and I had also taken one of ourselves, holding the camera out in front of us as we stuck our heads close together. Now I snapped one of the back of the truck as they left me with only the gassy exhaust fumes, and I told myself once again to stop caring.

In the motel room, I thought of calling Russell Berger to figure out what was going on so I could quit wondering. I knew his number by heart even though I'd only seen it that once. But I lost my nerve and called Ann instead—actually, I dialed her mother's cell since few Travelers had landlines. I could hear the air rushing by, and Ann said they were on their way to Macon.

"Where's Jimmy and Patrick?" she asked.

"Out."

"Oh."

"I hate it," I huffed. "I know what you're gonna say, but I hate it. Don't you ever wish it were different?"

"Like how?"

"Like maybe you weren't a Traveler and could just have boyfriends?"

"I guess that sounds kind of fun—I mean the boyfriends part." Ann paused. "But why do you even care? You've got a fiancé. That's better than a boyfriend."

"Is it?"

"What are you talking about, Bridget? Is there something my brother should know?"

"No," I said. "It's just, sometimes, when they go out—"

"You know what?" Ann's tone hardened. "I don't really want to hear it. Because from where I'm standing, you look like you got it pretty good. Patrick's one of the best Traveler men there are, and you know I'm not just saying that because he's my brother."

"I know," I said.

I thought that would be it, but Ann kept on going. "Look at me. Jimmy doesn't give a shit about me. Don't think I don't know that, because I do. And who's left? All the other guys are either taken or else they're losers or they don't ever want to be married. No one wants to even get matched up anymore. My dad says it's a sign that we're losing our heritage, that pretty soon we'll just be true gypsies and that's it, with no reason or rules or anything. It'll just be everybody out for themselves. So don't go acting all sad that you have to marry a great guy like Patrick because I don't want to hear it while I'm sitting here with nothing that good in my life."

"Okay," I said. I knew I should say more. But I was stunned. For all her romance writing and following Jimmy around, Ann was more realistic than I was. I kept hoping for something better with Patrick when I should've realized how good I had it already. I had no reason to bitch. Why did I think I deserved more? Why did I think life should be different for me? In fact, life was better for me than for most Traveler girls. So Patrick slept around a little. We weren't even married yet. He didn't drink that much, he never got violent with me, he hardly ever even raised his voice, and he worked hard.

"Listen, I gotta go," Ann muttered. "My mom needs the phone."

"I'm sorry," I pleaded, fingering the end of one of my braids and wishing I'd never brought it up in the first place.

"Sure," she said, like she either didn't believe me or didn't care.

I hung up and sat in the motel room with the noise of the TV coming from next door. I'd wash up and go to bed, wait for Jimmy and Patrick to stumble home. I'd read and tell myself I had it good; I'd think of Ann when I doubted it. But still I knew the thoughts would come. What if I wasn't a Traveler? What if I could choose my own boyfriends and not marry until years later, when I was ready? What if Mom and Dad didn't depend on my marrying good? What if? But that was the problem exactly—it was only *what if*. It wasn't reality. Reality was tomorrow—another day of selling people condos they wouldn't ever own.

chapter 15

There are only so many kinds of burritos you can eat before just looking at one makes you want to retch. For a change Jimmy and Patrick went out to pick up Chinese food for lunch. Big Jim was also out when the bell over the door jingled and a young couple walked in.

They looked barely older than Jimmy. He was wearing a crisp white polo shirt, and you could see through it to the tank top underneath and the silver chain and cross around his neck. She wore a pink floral-patterned tent of a dress and was very pregnant.

"Can I help you?" I asked in the polite tone I'd perfected over the last few weeks.

"Yes, we've got an appointment with Jim Flynn. The Cranes."

"That's for one-thirty, right?" I checked the appointment book just to make sure, but I always knew the day's schedule.

"I made him come early," the woman said.

The man laughed and put his arm around his wife. "She's a little bit excited, that's all."

"It just sounded so great in the ad," she gushed.

"Well, Mr. Flynn's out on another appointment. But he'll be back soon. Maybe he can fit you in early if you want to wait."

The woman looked hopefully at her husband, who nodded. "We'll wait."

I showed them to the conference table. The woman looked at the tall chair, palmed her stomach, and smiled at me. "I don't think that looks like the best idea for me right now."

"Oh my God, of course. I'll get you my chair."

"I can just stand," she said.

I rolled my chair over. "Absolutely not."

She sank down into it and sighed. "I'm Lizzy." She stuck out a pink-fingernailed hand for me to shake. "And this is my husband, Todd."

"Bridget."

"Nice to meet you, Bridget," Lizzy answered cheerfully.

I glanced at her stomach. "When's the baby due?"

Lizzy laughed. "Eight weeks. That's why we're eager to see the place. If we could just get somewhat moved in—"

Todd interrupted her. "I keep telling her the baby doesn't care when we move in."

"I care," Lizzy said to Todd. Then she explained, "It's our first baby . . . and our first place that we'll actually own. How perfect would that be, to have both of those things at the same time?" She smiled at the thought of it all coming together like that and then asked, "Have you seen them?"

"Oh yeah, they're beautiful. Really beautiful."

Lizzy looked from me to Todd. "I know this is going to be the place."

She explained that they'd been looking for a while, but either the homes weren't in a family neighborhood or they were way out of their price range. As she talked, I pictured Todd decorating the nursery, maybe putting glow-in-the-dark stars on the ceiling. Lizzy would hang curtains she sewed herself from a how-to instruction book. But I stopped myself and remembered. There would be no new place. They'd put down their money and then call us or stop by about some detail, like when the closing would be and when they'd be able to move in. We'd be long gone by then—by the time they realized they'd been had. And what would happen then? They'd probably move in with Todd's parents. The baby would sleep in their room, or they'd put the crib in the bathroom. It wasn't so horrible—they wouldn't be out on the street. I tried to come up with reasons why what we were doing to them wasn't cruel. I tried to think of things about them to laugh at, like Todd's wife-beater showing under his polo or the fact that Lizzy looked like a human bouquet. But even though those things were true, I couldn't hate the Cranes like I wanted to.

"Well, it might be a little small if you're thinking of having more kids," I said. "The units only have two bedrooms." I knew I should've kept my mouth shut, but how could I with them sitting there all hopeful and with a baby on the way?

Todd shrugged. "That's fine."

"For now," Lizzy added. "I mean, a baby has to have a brother or sister."

"If you're already thinking about that, maybe you should consider a bigger place," I cautioned. What was the harm in maybe saving just this one couple the heartache?

But Todd shook his head. "This is all we can do for now. In a few years things'll be different."

Lizzy leaned toward me. "Todd's working on his certificate in bookkeeping."

"Trucking's just for now," Todd added.

I forced a smile, but all of a sudden I felt sick. Here they were trying so hard to make life better and we were gonna fuck it all up for them. I couldn't stand looking at either of them anymore—at Todd's see-through shirt, Lizzy's floral bulging stomach, her perfect pink fingernails. I excused myself, saying I had work I needed to get back to.

The only problem was that I didn't have any work. I never had any work except answering questions when people called and setting up appointments. I was stuck reading magazines, newspapers, supermarket circulars—whatever I could get my hands on. There wasn't a bookstore in town, and I'd finished *Anne Frank*. Sometimes I'd stare out the window at the surrounding mountains and wish we had time to go see the Grand Canyon. It seemed crazy to go all the way to Arizona and not see the Grand Canyon.

I'd gotten so bored once that I'd written the thesis to what would've been my term paper on the Black Sox. It was pretty good—how the Black Sox and the baseball troubles in general paralleled the problems of society at large during that time. But it was late July now, and school was long out. Those term papers had all been handed in and graded, with mine missing. The sisters probably wondered whether I'd be back in the fall, but when I didn't show up they'd soon forget all about me. So would Mrs. C., who'd probably replaced me with someone older and more responsible.

When Jimmy and Patrick came back with the Chinese food, I introduced them to Todd and Lizzy. Jimmy put the steaming cartons on my desk, wiped his hands on his pants, a habit he hadn't been able to break, and then shook hands with them. He made some lame joke about being addicted to chicken fried rice and Todd and Lizzy laughed, but I could tell they didn't think it was funny.

I walked around to the back of the office and sat on the cement curb next to the Dumpster from the Mexican place that smelled of grease mixed with spoiled salsa. I hadn't smoked much since we'd come out here, mostly because Patrick hated it. But right now there was nothing I needed more. Stealing from Kmart and Wal-Mart was different because you never really saw who you stole from. And those chains made so much money that a couple hundred dollars here or there didn't matter. Even with the trailers Mom sold, even then, hell, at least the people had a trailer. They just paid more for it. But these people would spend all they had and walk away with nothing.

Three cigarettes later Patrick came to tell me he and Jimmy were taking Todd and Lizzy to see the condos. "This one's a done deal, I know it. Chalk up deposit number seven."

When I didn't respond, Patrick playfully poked me. "Number seven. That's thirty-five grand. Isn't that great?"

I shrugged and dragged on my cigarette. My stomach felt like the butt looked when I inhaled—fire-red and ashy. Why did I think of Todd and Lizzy but Patrick didn't?

"You're ready to go home, aren't you?" he asked.

I exhaled, watching the line of smoke fade away. "Do you ever feel weird? Showing a condo that's a lie?"

Patrick answered me right away, like it was simple. "You can't."

"But don't you ever? I mean, what about Todd and Lizzy? They're so young, and what if they put down all they have?" When we'd talked about the Black Sox, Patrick said he couldn't believe anyone would fix the World Series. But this was life we were fixing—someone's life. Why was it any different?

"We have to make a living just like anybody," he said.

"I don't know. . . ."

Patrick must've thought about it before because he had answers ready. And not stupid answers either, like that they deserve it if they're that dumb.

"You think we're different, but we're not," he continued. "There's lots of people make a living like we do. Like take stockbrokers. They call people up and sell them stocks they know are gonna tank."

The look on my face must've told Patrick I wasn't convinced yet because he kept going.

"And what about insurance companies? They make people pay year after year to protect themselves from something terrible, and then when something happens, more often than not they won't pay for it. They find some reason why they don't have to."

I remembered seeing a program on one of those news magazine shows. Some man's insurance company wouldn't pay for his five-year-old daughter to have a special treatment she needed to live. They were just going to let her die. But just because the world was full of people doing shitty things to make a buck, did that mean we should do it too?

"You can't think too much about it," Patrick said. "I know what you're saying. But you just can't think about it."

I wished I could be like him. Like Ann. Like everybody else. I wished I didn't care about Todd and Lizzy or, even better, that I could sit here with Patrick and just laugh at them.

"I gotta go," Patrick said. "Jimmy's waiting."

I nodded. Patrick reached out and lifted my chin. "I know it's hard being so far away from home."

He was trying to make me feel better. It was sweet of him, but he just didn't get it. "But we're always far away from home. We don't even have homes."

"Sure we do. Home is wherever we all are."

"But that's all over. Don't you ever get sick of it? Of moving from town to town? Of picking up and leaving just when you get used to a place?"

Patrick looked at me like I was crazy. "Are you kidding? That's the best part. It never gets boring."

"Who says being normal has to be boring?"

"Who says we're not normal?" Patrick answered.

"We're not. Normal people go to school and have normal jobs."

"And have a normal boss breathing down their necks all the time. How would you like that? I'll tell you, I wouldn't. There's nothing like the freedom of the road, of knowing you make all the decisions."

But I didn't make the decisions. And neither did Patrick, although someday he would. But I never would, not really.

Patrick stepped away from me. "We'll be home soon," he said.

I forced a smile, knowing that home, if it existed at all, wasn't the answer.

chapter 16

ridget, right?"

I looked up from the article I was reading in *Glamour* on how to win your man back when he's gone astray to see Mr. Ruby walk through the door, the hitch in his walk more noticeable than when I'd met him, rain dripping from his dark green slicker.

"Yes," I said, surprised he remembered my name. "What can I do for you?"

Mr. Ruby peeled off his slicker. "I had a few questions and I just thought I'd stop by."

"You shouldn't be driving in this weather," I said. "You should've just called."

Mr. Ruby shrugged. "Can't let a little rain slow you down."

"Well, I guess some others thought the same because Jim's out showing the units right now, and so are Jimmy and Patrick." It was true—business *had* picked up.

Mr. Ruby smiled. "That's all right. I'm sure you can help me."

"I don't know. I know you came all this way, but I really just make the appointments."

There were certain questions I could answer, but Big Jim had made it clear that with any others I should always get him. Mr. Ruby had already seen the condo, so he knew the answers to questions like *"Do all the units have two bathrooms?"* or *"Does each unit have a dishwasher?"*

"Don't sell yourself short," Mr. Ruby scolded me.

I smiled. "I'll see if I can help."

Mr. Ruby pulled a chair up next to my desk and laced his fingers together. "I'll be honest with you. The condo is perfect for me. Perfect. But since you all are contractual Realtors, I'll be left dealing with the company that built the units, so I want to know a little bit more about them. Is this a company you all have dealt with before?"

"Yes," I answered, weaving what I thought was a solid lie. "We sold condos for them in Austin and in Tucson."

"Okay, so you'll probably know this—will they be doing the managing of the building or are they hiring a management company?"

"They do the managing," I said confidently.

"Really?" Mr. Ruby asked.

Shit. What if Big Jim had already told him something else? I'd planned on playing dumb, listening to Mr. Ruby's questions, and then telling him I was sorry, I couldn't help him. Now I had the terrible feeling I was digging my own grave, only it wouldn't just be my grave, it would be Big Jim's and Jimmy's and Patrick's too. And why? Maybe it was the combination of *not* wanting to act dumb because it might seem suspicious, not wanting to act dumb period—especially in front of Mr. Ruby, who thought I was smart—and wanting to help Mr. Ruby out that made me answer his questions even though I heard Big Jim in my head telling me not to. "I mean, they usually do the managing." I backpedaled as fast as I could. "But we should check with Jim just to make sure. Why don't you wait here? I can page him and have him come right over."

Did I sound worried? Or like I was covering something up? I didn't know what was happening to me. Usually I could do this. Usually I was good.

Mr. Ruby checked his watch. "Actually, I'm headed to the doctor's." He nodded toward his right leg. "This damn leg is acting up again with all the rain we've had. Shrapnel—avoid it if you can."

Mr. Ruby eased out of the chair, slid back into his still-dripping slicker, and headed to the door. "Keep studying, Bridget," he called over the jingle of the bell.

After Mr. Ruby left, I looked out at the rain. I was glad to be in Arizona right then and not someplace where I had to think about all the driveways and roofs we'd done. But I did have to think about Mr. Ruby's questions. Was he suspicious or just asking things a person would ask if they were going to buy a condo? I wasn't sure, but I decided I better tell Big Jim all about Mr. Ruby's visit when he came back.

Only when he came back, Big Jim hulked straight to his office without even saying hello. He holed up in there all afternoon, and when Jimmy and Patrick came back they told me his ex-wife had called. He hadn't told them anything more, but it was clear that whatever she had called about had pissed him off good.

That night the three of them went out again, leaving me back at the motel. In the room, I took a bath—something I did every night if I could. I lay back and wondered whether Mr. Ruby knew something and why he'd been able to shake me so easily. Had I let pride trip me up like Big Jim warned us about? I'd thought for sure his comments were meant for Jimmy, but then Mr. Ruby came along and said I was smart. Was I that pathetic, that saying I was smart was all it took? I vowed I'd tell Big Jim everything in the morning.

I was in bed watching a TV movie around ten-thirty when I heard a knock at the door. Jimmy had a key. Unless he was so drunk he'd lost it, he wouldn't be knocking. And it was too early for him to come home anyway. I wasn't about to swing the door wide open to some murderer, but then I heard Patrick's voice through the door. "Bridget, it's me."

"What're you doing here?" I climbed out of bed and opened the door, realizing as I did that I was only wearing underwear and a T-shirt that fell to midthigh.

"Couldn't stop thinking about you, I guess." Patrick moved toward me and kissed me. "Left them at the bar and hitched back."

Patrick's blue eyes were clear, and his face was its usual summer color, a few shades darker than pale. He wasn't drunk as far as I could tell. But maybe he was a little gone because he was bolder than usual. He kissed me again and we moved to the bed. With Jimmy and Big Jim at the bar we didn't have to worry about getting caught. He lay on top of me and I felt him against me through his pants. The power of his manliness, as Ann would've said. He slid his hand under my T-shirt. I didn't have a bra on, and I think it surprised him because his body pulsed and he breathed in, short and shallow. His hand felt smooth as it glided over my bare skin.

He was determined in a way he'd never been before, but I wasn't scared—not like with Jared. I wanted it to happen this time. Maybe if it did—if we did—then Patrick wouldn't need other girls anymore. Maybe us finally coming together and loving each other in this new way would once and for all answer the questions I still had about the *M* word.

I was ready, ready for whatever the next step was. But just when I thought something more might happen, Patrick rolled off me onto his back. He inhaled sharply, held it, then exhaled through his nose.

I couldn't believe it. With no one around to worry about and me obviously into it, he was stopping? "Don't you want to?"

"Of course I want to, but you know we can't," he said. "It'll be soon enough."

Patrick pulled me to him. I lay with my head on his chest, moving with each breath he took. My hand shaking, I reached for his belt and started to unbuckle it. I wanted to. I wanted to be the only one.

Patrick pushed my hand away. "I said no."

His words stung worse than if he'd hit me. He'd sleep with all those other girls but he wouldn't with me? Wouldn't with the one he was supposed to marry? The one he was supposed to love? That was bad enough, but Patrick went and made it worse.

"I'm not gonna mess this up just for something we can wait for. Say someone found out and it got back to your dad. My dad's counting on the bride-price."

I jolted up and stared at Patrick, wondering if I knew him at all. This was what it came down to. Patrick didn't want to sleep with me because his father was counting on the money. I'd been willing to risk everything—to give him myself, to risk my virginity, the one thing that made me marriageable—and he'd turned me away for money. Maybe money was why he was marrying me after all, not love. Maybe he'd much rather marry some other, prettier Traveler girl who didn't think as much and didn't want to go to school and didn't care about anything she wasn't supposed to care about.

"That's what this is about?" I yelled. "The bride-price?"

"Come on, Bridget," Patrick pleaded.

"No! I won't come on. Tell me how much. How much did he get for me? I hope it was a good price, at least."

Patrick sat up and rubbed his forehead. "I don't even know."

"Bullshit!" I boomed. "You know, so just say it. Did I get you and your dad a good chunk of change? Or could you've done better with some other girl?" I couldn't stand it. I was another job, another scam, another rip-off where the only thing that counted was how much the take was.

"Would you stop this?" Patrick begged.

I stood up. "Get out!" I shouted.

"What?" Patrick said, stunned.

"You heard me."

"Bridget—"

I didn't care what happened, what Dad or Mom said. There was no way I was marrying Patrick now. It was done. It was over. "Get out of here!" I screamed.

Patrick shook his head, then started for the door. But he turned back to me once more. "I wish you wouldn't be like this. You don't understand. It's just my dad—"

"I understand fine," I said.

After Patrick left, I bolted the door. I'd have to undo it later to let Jimmy in, but right then I needed to lock it. Goddamn Patrick. Every time I let him in just a little bit, he hurt me. Before he'd always been able to crawl back in somehow. But this was too much. There was no way I could ever forgive him.

chapter 17

Deposit 7—Todd and Lizzy's—came in the next day. Numbers 8 and 9 rolled in the day after that. I still wasn't talking to Patrick and didn't think I ever would. The minute we got home I was going to tell Mom and Dad that if they wanted me to marry Patrick they'd have to kill me first because I wasn't doing it alive.

Not talking to Patrick made it kind of hard at work. When he was there, I wouldn't look at him, and when someone called, I'd put them on hold, and instead of yelling "Patrick!" like I usually did, I just yelled, "Phone!"

When Patrick and Jimmy headed out to show the units around midmorning, Patrick put a book on my desk, *Shoeless Joe*. There was a note sticking out of it. It read: *I'm sorry. Let's talk.*

If Patrick thought it was that easy, he had another thing coming. He could have given me a whole library, he could have given me the entire 1919 Black Sox team back from the dead, and I wouldn't have cared, and I sure as hell wasn't going to listen to anything he had to say because there was nothing that'd make me hate him less.

He called an hour later, whispering my name, and I thought it was because he didn't want Jimmy to hear. I was about to hang up when he said softly, *"Misli."* Leave. His voice was urgent and trembling. *"Shayjo."* Police.

Patrick didn't need to say anything more. Those two Cant words were enough.

The phone clicked and I was left with silence. My heart raced, and the office felt strangely still. All I could think of was Mr. Ruby. With everything that'd happened with Patrick, I'd totally forgotten about telling Big Jim.

I tried to think if there was anything I could do now to help. But Big Jim was smart—he didn't leave paperwork or any traces of who we really were lying around. I had the disposable camera in my purse. That was the only evidence I could think of. I waited for a few more moments, just looking at the office— the fake world we'd created. Then I grabbed my jacket, my purse, and my cigarettes and split. There was no time to go back to the motel and get the rest of my stuff. That'd be asking for it. It was a ten-minute walk to town and I walked slowly. If I ran or looked worried, the cops might pick me up too. Maybe they were already looking for me.

At the bus station I bought a ticket on the next bus to any-where, which turned out to be Tucson. It was only a few hours' ride, and I called Mom when I got there, making sure no one was around to listen. I didn't think someone would've followed me, but you never knew.

"There's been trouble," I said, my voice breaking.

I told her how Patrick had called and that all I knew was that the cops had come. I didn't tell her anything about Mr. Ruby. I couldn't face that yet. I couldn't face admitting that for the second time I'd put others in danger.

"Oh God, Jimmy," Mom cried.

"I know," I said.

Mom was stunned and not thinking straight, so I did the thinking for her. I'd already checked the schedule. There was a bus headed to Tupelo in a half hour. Last time I'd talked to her had been a few days ago, and they'd been in Georgia. "Can you meet me in Tupelo tomorrow?" I asked.

"Yes," Mom managed. "We'll be there."

I walked outside to wait for the bus. It was a small station with a few benches and a rusty garbage can with more garbage outside of it than inside. There were only two other people waiting: a middle-aged woman with her hair tied back in a bandanna clutching a straw bag in her lap and a younger man with a quarter inch of stubble on his head and a guitar case ducttaped shut. I went to the one empty bench and sat down. I thought if I closed my eyes maybe I could shut the world out for a few seconds, but I knew I shouldn't at a place like this.

Piped-in music played over the PA, and I was half listening when the song changed to one that sounded so beautiful. The lyrics began quiet, low, like someone humming softly to themselves. It wasn't until midway through that I really heard the words and thought of Patrick. The Allman Brothers sang about crossing roads, going all over, but always coming back to sweet Melissa.

It hit me then that Patrick's first thought had been of me. Not of getting himself out, but of getting to me in time. Just when I thought I'd thrown him out forever, he'd pushed his way back into my heart again.

Mom was in the truck waiting for me in Tupelo when the bus pulled in. I opened the truck door to her red, puffy eyes. I'd sort of expected Dad to be there too, but when I saw just Mom, I wondered what I'd been thinking. Of course Dad wasn't going to come. After warning everyone how the whole thing was a bad idea in the first place, he'd be too pissed to come. Mom reached over and hugged me, sobbing into my shoulder.

"I'm so glad you're okay," she said.

"What about Jimmy and Patrick? Have you heard anything?"

Mom sniffled and swallowed before speaking. "Jimmy called. They've been arrested. Big Jim too." My last hope faded as Mom told me Big Jim and Jimmy had been outside when the cops showed up. Patrick had spotted the cops cuffing them from inside one of the condos. After calling me, he'd snuck out the back, but they'd caught him too.

"What's gonna happen?" I asked. "Will they get off?"

"I don't know," Mom sighed. "The arraignment's tomorrow. Hopefully they'll set bail."

She started crying again. "Your father says maybe prison is what he needs. Even if bail's set, he says maybe we shouldn't post it."

"He's not serious," I said, but I wasn't so sure.

Mom cleared her throat. "I don't know. But I do know I can't take much more of this. Jimmy and him going at it all the time. I go to bed every night and I pray for things to be okay between them."

When we pulled into the campground and up to the trailer, I opened the door and was about to climb out when Mom stopped me. "Wait," she whispered. Then we both heard it— Dad cursing wildly from inside the trailer.

"That goddamn fool—goddamn *yonk*—or no, *you're* the fool. *You're* the one who let him go in the first place. Should never have listened to that two-bit no-good hustler *yonk* even if he is your damn brother."

Mom turned to me. "Go on over to Ann's. Spend the night and come back in the morning."

I looked at Mom, thinking maybe I shouldn't leave her alone. She must have read my mind because she said, "Go. He'll settle down soon."

The Murphys were a few trailers away, and just before I got there a loud crash boomed from the direction of our trailer. I winced but kept walking.

I knocked on the Murphys' door. We'd only been gone a few weeks but it felt like forever, and I was glad Ann hadn't changed. She was the same old Ann with her curly hair and beautiful smile.

"I'm so glad you're all right," she said, hugging me tight.

"I'm fine."

"Can you believe this?"

"Did you talk to Patrick?"

"Yeah. He called—his one phone call, I guess."

"And he's okay?"

Ann nodded.

I thought again of Patrick's *first* phone call. How I'd been his first thought. "If he hadn't called me, maybe he'd have gotten out." I shuddered.

"If he hadn't called you, they would have arrested you at the office," Ann said.

But it didn't make me feel better. I almost wished I'd been arrested too. At least then I wouldn't have felt so guilty. "Did you hear anything about who tipped off the cops?" I quaked, waiting for Ann's response.

"Some cop saw the office and the condos and got suspicious. Patrick said he brought his pregnant wife and posed as a couple looking to buy."

I gasped.

"What's wrong?" Ann asked.

I shook my head. "Nothing. I just never would have guessed that . . ." I thought I was so good at pegging people, at figuring out who they were just by looking at them. I thought we all were. But this time they'd gotten us at our own game. And was I really good at pegging people anyway? Every time I thought I had someone pegged—Jimmy, for not caring about anybody but himself; Patrick, for loving or not loving me; Ann, for living in a dreamworld—they surprised me.

"Listen," Ann said. "I'm sorry about the other night when you called. I didn't know what you wanted me to say, and then I just got going—"

"It's all right," I answered, looking right at her. If anyone should've been sorry, it was me. "Don't worry about it, okay?"

Ann nodded. "I'm worried about *them*."

"Me too," I said.

chapter 18

Y our father wants to talk to you" was the first thing Mom said when I got back the next morning. She sat at the card table in her robe, her hands wrapped around a jumbo glass of iced coffee. I was relieved to see that she looked fine. A little tired, but fine.

"What about?"

Before Mom could answer, Dad stumbled out of the trailer. He still had his work clothes on from the day before, and now they were crumpled as well as dirty. His right hand was bandaged up. He'd smashed something, but I figured I should be glad Dad smashed *things* when he got mad and not Mom or me.

There was no *"Glad you're safe"* or *"Good to have you home"* from Dad. Only "You're to marry Patrick next month."

I started to speak, but he cut me off, his voice growing louder and more firm. "That's the way it's gotta be. Now more than ever. And I don't want to hear anything else about it. I've had it with you and Jimmy both. I'm telling you, I've had it. You'll listen to me and you'll do what I say."

Dad turned and stomped back into the trailer, leaving Mom and me alone. She looked at me pleadingly. "It's not the ideal time of year and it'll be smaller than we'd like, but we'll make sure it's a nice ceremony."

As if the size of the wedding or what relatives came mattered to me. "You think it's okay to just sell me off like that?" I snapped back at her. "What about what I want? What about me? How could you let him do this?"

I walked to Mom and snatched her cell phone from where it lay faceup in front of her on the card table. "Who's Russell Berger? Why have you been lying to me?"

"Bridget," Mom said, trembling. "You don't understand."

"No, I don't!" I yelled. "Because you won't tell me. Because you don't think I'm old enough to know. Well, I'm old enough, okay? I'm old enough."

Taking Mom's phone, I tore away from the trailer. Mom called after me, but I kept running. I stopped by a rusted-out trailer that someone had parked and never come back for. If Mom wouldn't tell me the truth, then I'd find out for myself.

I dialed Russell Berger's number. A woman answered: "Mom, what's happening? Is Jimmy okay?"

I couldn't speak.

"Mom? Are you okay?"

This much I knew: the woman had caller ID and recognized that I was calling from Mom's phone. But why she was calling Mom "Mom" and knew about Jimmy, I couldn't for the life of me figure out.

"Who—who are you?" I sputtered.

She gasped slightly at the sound of my voice and then said softly, "Bridget? Bridget, is that you? It's me, Winnie. . . ."

I turned the name over in my mind, but if it sounded

familiar it was only because it was a common Traveler name. "Winnie who?"

"Winnie your sister."

"I don't have a sister," I replied quickly. I repeated her name again and again in my head, trying to make sense of it and what she was telling me, but I couldn't.

"You don't remember me, do you?" she asked. "You were pretty young when I left. I've missed you, Bridget. You and Jimmy both."

"I don't believe you," I stammered, sure this was some kind of scam. "Who are you? What kind of shit are you trying to pull?"

"I'm not trying to pull—" She sighed. "It's the truth. I *am* your sister."

"Prove it," I said.

"Your birthday is January twenty-second and Jimmy's is March fourteenth."

"Anyone can find that shit out. Can't you do any better than that?"

"You go to St. Jude's, where I used to go. Mom says you always have your nose in a book. She also says you're not sure about marrying Patrick. You used to like Rocky Road ice cream even though you picked out the marshmallows and the chocolate chips. . . . God, Bridget, I left when you were three. I don't know what else you want from me."

"I believe you," I said finally, barely managing to get the words out. It wasn't the details. Anyone could have figured out that stuff. But she kept talking, kept trying to prove it. Someone trying a scam would have just hung up.

"But why?" I asked. "Why would you leave?"

"I fell in love with a Country boy." Winnie paused. "Well,

I guess I'm full-fledged Country myself now," she laughed. "Dad said if I didn't give him up and marry a Traveler, I'd have to leave and he'd disown me, and I couldn't give Russ up. Like I said, you were young, I'm not surprised you don't remember."

So it was Winnie who'd fallen in love with a Country man, not Mom. It was never Mom. And all the calls weren't about Jimmy and Jared or drugs either. That was why Jimmy was so sure about it all but didn't want to tell me. He obviously knew about Winnie. And for that matter so did Big Jim. That was what he hadn't wanted to talk about at the steak house. Losing her daughter had made Mom tough. And all the calls over the years that Mom had claimed were business, all her warnings not to mess with her phone—it was all because of Winnie, because she didn't want me to know.

And now I had a sister. I said it to myself a few times, and as I did, more than anger at Mom or Jimmy for not telling me, there was another feeling. A feeling like all of a sudden I had something more in my life, some*one* more. For all our differences, Jimmy and I did share a strong bond. But to have a sister. Someone so much more like myself. Someone who'd gone through what I was going through.

"What do you look like?" I asked. "Do you look like me?" I didn't know why it mattered, but I wanted a picture of her in my mind.

"Mom sent me a snapshot of you and Jimmy once, but that was a while ago, so I don't really know what you look like. I guess I'm pretty tall. I have Mom's dark hair. Mine's long. I keep saying I'm going to cut it all off, but I haven't."

I looked up at the bright orange sun against the blue sky that looked like a kid's crayon drawing.

"There's so much I want to talk to you about. I want to

know everything about you," Winnie said. "Is Jimmy okay? Last time I talked to Mom she said you were on a bus headed home and he'd been arrested."

"We haven't heard anything else. The arraignment's today." I paused. "What about Dad? He still won't talk to you?"

Winnie sighed. "Won't talk to me or even about me. Mom brought it up with him once. It was a long time ago, but long enough since I'd left. He flipped out. I guess that's the way it's got to be. I used to hate him for it. I hated him for keeping me from existing to you, even if he didn't want me around. But I've come to see he's just trying to hold everything together—our way of life."

"I guess so," I said, noticing that Winnie said *our* and not *your.*

I was quiet, just thinking about it all, about how in only a few minutes so many of my questions had been answered, yet now I had a whole set of new ones. Finally Winnie said, "You must be exhausted. Let's talk again soon. Call anytime. Call collect. And let me know when you hear anything about Jimmy, okay?"

"Okay," I managed to say.

"And, Bridget," Winnie added, "take care of yourself."

I hung up and wiped away the sweat that trickled down my cheek from where I'd been clutching the phone to my ear. With the glare of the sun hitting me full on, I walked back to the trailer. What Dad had said about marrying Patrick next month was the furthest thing from my mind now. The only thing I was thinking about was Winnie. And Mom. Knowing about Winnie jumbled all the things I knew about Mom. Losing Winnie was why she was terrified of losing Jimmy. Losing Winnie was why she loved him so much. Maybe losing Winnie was also why Dad was scared of what would happen if I didn't marry Patrick soon.

Mom was still at the card table when I got back, and Dad's truck was gone. The heat was getting to her too; she'd opened the neck of her robe wide. She must have seen from my face that I knew because she nodded and then smiled.

"Why didn't you tell me?" I asked.

"I wanted to. Sometimes I look at you and—" Mom teared up. "You just look so much like her."

"You should have told me."

Mom shook her head. "It's not that simple. I know how everything looks to you—black-and-white. But it's not. Sometimes there're things you don't want to do, but you have to do them. You have to. I couldn't be sure you'd keep quiet. Your father doesn't know I talk to her, and he can't know—you got it?"

"Yes."

Mom stood up and took a tentative step toward me. "You'll understand someday. When you have children of your own, you'll understand." She pulled me close. "You and Jimmy are all I've got," she whispered. "I love you both so much."

It was then that I folded into her in a way that I hadn't been able to in a long, long time.

chapter 19

"As long as you're sitting around, you might as well help out," Dad said.

After the arraignment, Patrick and Jimmy called to say that since they had no priors the judge set bail at fifteen thousand dollars for each of them. Big Jim wasn't as lucky. With his long list of priors, bail was denied, and he was awaiting trial. Dad called a bail bondsman about Jimmy and Patrick. The way it worked was you paid ten percent of the amount of bail and then the bail bondsman posted the full amount. Dad paid the fifteen hundred dollars for Jimmy, and he paid for Patrick too. Then Patrick and Jimmy were supposed to stick around for the trial. Only the minute they were free on bail, they skipped out, lifted a new truck, and headed to Tupelo to meet us.

I hadn't gone along with Dad on jobs since I was really young. Back then he'd tell whoever owned the driveway or roof he was hoping to work on that Mom was sick and I was riding along with him so I'd be out of her hair for the day. The illnesses he gave Mom ranged from the flu to something more tragic, based on whether Dad thought the people looked easy or hard to convince—whether the sympathy card was necessary.

"I think I'll stay here," I told him. Even though I understood a little better why Dad was tightening his grip on me, I was still pissed at him. And now I was also mad at him for keeping Winnie from me, from all of us, for so many years.

Dad nodded to the truck. "Come on. With Patrick not around, I need your help."

"Fine," I muttered. I'd go. But I wouldn't be happy about it. Dad probably thought we'd bond and then everything would be fine between us again. But there was no way that was happening.

It was a half-hour drive to the neighborhood Dad had cased the day before. The houses were small but well kept—flower boxes in the windows, trimmed lawns. If people let their houses fall apart, never painting them, never watering the lawn or trimming bushes, they wouldn't care about what shape their roof or driveway was in. We went after people who cared enough but didn't have the money to hire a regular company.

Dad nosed the truck alongside a tan house with a driveway full of dips and craters. I waited in the car as Dad headed up the stone walkway and knocked on the door. An older woman—Mrs. Forbes, I figured from the name in bold capital letters on the mailbox—answered. She wore long pants and a long-sleeved shirt even though it was Africa hot out, and she balanced most of her weight on a metal cane. Dad pointed to the driveway, then motioned to the truck. Even though I couldn't hear him, I knew every word he was saying.

"I just did a driveway up the street for one of your neighbors." He'd use a name from a mailbox up the road. *"The Pierces? Well, I was driving by when I saw your driveway. I hope you don't mind*

165

me noticing, but it really looks like it could use repaving. So I said to myself . . ."

And here's where he probably used me.

"Actually, when I said that your driveway looked like it'd seen better days, it was my daughter who said, 'Dad, don't we have extra sealant in the tanks?' See, my daughter knows that every day when I get home, I throw away all the extra because it's no good the next day."

Mrs. Forbes, who might be a widow or maybe her husband was just out, would ask Dad about pricing. She'd think she was being smart, doing what her husband always told her to do, asking questions so you don't agree to something only to find out after the job's done that it cost an arm and a leg. Dad would tell her that since he was going to throw out the extra sealant anyway, he'd only charge her for the labor. He'd give her a deal. She'd agree either because she didn't have a husband to take care of her anymore and here was a man looking out for her or because her husband would be so impressed by the deal she'd gotten when he came home.

She must've agreed because Dad walked back to the truck and started unhooking the hoses. He came to my window and said, "You just gonna sit there or you gonna give your old man a hand?"

Dad and I worked side by side on the driveway. I'd spray the sealant and he'd smooth it into place. Aside from exchanging a few words about doing this section next or putting a little more sealant there, we didn't speak. I'd forgotten how hot it was working on blacktop. I thought of Winnie and how she'd probably helped Dad pave driveways when she was young too. She could probably still remember the heavy smell of the sealant, the soreness in your shoulders when you woke up the next morning, even though her life was completely different now. I hadn't asked her what she did for a living. Whether she'd gone to school in Boston. She'd probably finished high school. Maybe she'd gone to college.

When the last patch of the driveway was the shiny black color of all the rest, Dad leaned over his rake. He pulled a handkerchief out of his pants pocket and wiped the streaming sweat off his forehead. When he'd stuffed the handkerchief back in his pocket, he set his gaze on me. "You know I wouldn't pick a husband for you if I didn't think he wasn't going to do right by you."

Dad's hair was dark with sweat and his shirt was soaked through. This was how he had looked coming home every single day for as long as I could remember. Day after day it was driveways, roofs, maybe painting a barn every now and then. But he never got sick of it, or if he did, he never complained. Days when he made nothing and days when he made thousands of dollars all seemed the same. Days that were spent inside because of weather or because there was no work left him restless, edgy. For all Dad's faults, in many ways he was a good man. A good husband to Mom. Even a good father. He was just trying his best.

"I know," I said. I wished that was the only reason Dad had chosen Patrick for me. But I knew he'd also chosen him for himself. For the work Patrick would do. For how he could take care of all of us later on.

"Patrick's a fine man, and he'll be a fine husband to you. He'll treat you right. I'll see to that, don't you worry about it for a second."

"I'm not worried." I didn't doubt Patrick would take good care of me. It was just whether I wanted to be taken care of. But I couldn't explain that to Dad.

Dad straightened and started toward the truck. I stopped him by asking, "Dad, what's gonna happen when Jimmy comes home?"

"That depends," Dad answered.

"On what?"

"On Jimmy."

I thought of Winnie—how it must have hurt him to lose her. How he didn't want to lose Jimmy that same way. I wanted to tell him to just let up on Jimmy a little—to not ride him so hard. But it didn't feel like my place to say it, and then Dad took the hose from me and hauled it and the rake to the truck and the moment had passed. I waited in the driveway while Dad wiped down the nozzle of the hose and the handle of the rake and secured the hose in its spool.

As Dad walked back toward the house, Mrs. Forbes opened the screen door. "I've made some lemonade for y'all," she called out.

Her kitchen was small, and framed needlepoint sayings like KISS THE COOK and THOSE WHO MAKE BREAD SELDOM LOAF covered the walls. She motioned us to the round wooden table and hobbled to the fridge. She rested her hand on the counter and, propping herself up, opened the fridge and took out a big plastic jug of pink lemonade. She poured two tall glasses, her bony hands shaking so that a little of the lemonade spilled on the counter.

I rose from my seat and took the glasses back to the table for her.

"Thank you, dear," she said, and joined us at the table.

Dad nodded toward the driveway through the kitchen window. "Looks a lot better now, doesn't it?"

"It does indeed. Thanks to you and your lovely daughter

here." She turned to me and put a surprisingly cool hand on my wrist. "Aren't you nice to help out your father. I used to love helping my father in the fields. We had a farm in Wisconsin. He even let me drive the tractor. That may not seem like much to you now, but back when I was young, girls didn't drive tractors."

I smiled and sipped my lemonade. Everyone loved to tell their story. The lemonade was sour—needed about ten heaping spoonfuls of sugar. Dad gulped his whole glass down and wiped his mouth with the back of his hand.

He held up his empty glass. "That was some lemonade."

"Let me get you some more," Mrs. Forbes offered.

But before she strained to get up, I told her I'd get it for her.

"Aren't you a dear," she said to me, and then to Dad, "Aren't you lucky to have this girl to help you."

"I'm actually on summer break from college," I said as I filled Dad's glass again. "That's why I'm around. I'm studying history."

Mrs. Forbes nodded. "My late husband—may he rest in peace—loved to read any and all books about history. He'd read about this and that president—Roosevelt was his favorite. Of course, Jack Kennedy was my favorite." Mrs. Forbes's face lit up and she even blushed. "But Teddy Roosevelt—you ever study anything about him?"

"Actually, I'm taking a course on him next semester," I replied.

"Bridget's a good student, all right," Dad added.

He thought I was just playing—and I was—but there was a truth to my act that Dad didn't see. The truth that maybe I wanted that from my life—to go to school, to study history. But Dad just thought I was making small talk like we always did, charming her so that she'd tip us and wouldn't have a fit when Dad jacked up the price for the job.

We chitchatted a little longer before Dad must've thought it was enough. "Well, we should really get out of your hair and get on our way."

Mrs. Forbes waved him off with a fluttering hand. "You're not in my hair. It's nice to have someone to talk with."

Dad downed the last inch of his lemonade. "Still, we should be getting home to the missus."

"Well, okay, if you have to go, then let me get your money. You said a hundred and fifty?"

"Actually, it took a little longer than we thought," Dad said. "Let's say two hundred."

Mrs. Forbes nodded. "Fair enough. You *were* out there a good long time."

With a hand on the kitchen table, she pushed herself out of her chair and motioned to where her cane rested against the door frame. "Can you hand me my cane, dear? I'll go upstairs and get the money for you." Mrs. Forbes let out a sad little laugh. "I'm not as spry on the stairs as I used to be. My son wants me to go into one of those homes, but I told him I'll sleep down here before I do that."

Dad eyed me but I glanced away. "Well, no need to tire yourself going all the way up the stairs," he offered. "Bridget can get it for you if you tell her where it is."

I hoped Mrs. Forbes would say no, but she didn't hesitate. "That would be great," she sighed. She told me that I'd find her "bank" in the bottom drawer of her dresser and to count out $225.

"A tip isn't necessary," Dad said.

"No, you worked hard out there. I saw you."

I moved toward the stairs without looking back. If I didn't make eye contact with Dad, I could pretend I didn't know what I should do. I was at the first step when Dad called my name and I *had* to look back.

"Take off your shoes. I don't want you getting this nice lady's house all dirty."

Dad's eyes spoke what he couldn't say aloud in front of Mrs. Forbes. There was no way around it. I couldn't claim I didn't know what he wanted.

I took off my sneakers and climbed the stairs, which creaked and groaned under me. Mrs. Forbes's bedroom was on my right at the top. A beautiful handmade quilt covered her bed, and the dresser was old and well made. Above it hung framed black-and-white photos: a wedding shot, baby pictures, a man in uniform.

I opened the bottom drawer of the dresser and found an old dark-stained wooden box. The gold nameplate on the top read FOR IRIS, ALWAYS, JAKE. The drawer smelled wonderful, like dried flowers, and I paused, breathing the scent in before opening the box.

Inside I found a bunch of bills with a thick blue rubber band around them. I took the roll out and undid the rubber band. I counted out the money onto the hooked rug on the floor. Some of the bills were well worn, thin under my fingers. A few were crisp, bright in color. Each bill probably came from a different place and time—money she'd saved for who knew how many years. All told, there was three thousand dollars.

Patrick or Jimmy would've taken it all. Ann would've too. Dad expected me to. It was the type of find, the type of luck, that made a day extraordinary. Not that Dad would brag about those days to cousins or friends like others did. But it was still a day that meant we could put money away, perhaps put some into stocks until we needed it for something bigger than everyday needs—a wedding, a funeral, bailing Jimmy and Patrick out like we'd just done. We wouldn't blow it on just anything. We needed that money too.

But I couldn't do it. Even though I knew Dad was counting on me, I just couldn't take this poor woman's savings. I couldn't stand the thought of her coming up here, pausing between steps to catch her breath, finally opening her box to find we'd cleaned her out. She'd cry and think of how nice we'd been and then think how stupid, stupid, stupid she'd been to trust us. She'd cry for her husband and for getting old and for not being able to make it up the damn stairs anymore. She'd be too ashamed to tell her son, but she'd need the money for her prescriptions. Maybe she'd even think about dying. Letting herself fall down those stairs she could barely walk up anymore. Ending it all because life was too sad and the people who'd stopped by and made that life less sad for a minute or two with just simple conversation turned out to be thieves.

I took three hundred dollars and that was it. Mrs. Forbes might not even notice the extra seventy-five dollars missing. And it was enough that Dad might believe me when I told him that was all there was.

chapter 20

Winnie had said to call her collect, and I did the next day after I'd walked to the convenience store where I'd dropped off the film from Arizona. Before calling I sat on the curb by the pay phone and looked at the photos: me next to the cactus, reaching out a wary hand to touch one of the spikes; Jimmy just waking up; Patrick in the cowboy hat. Then there was the one Patrick and I had taken of ourselves. We were so close to the lens that we looked distorted, our smiles too wide, our noses too big. I wanted to smile or laugh, like people were supposed to when they looked at photos, but knowing what had happened in Arizona, I just couldn't.

After looking through the pictures, I went into the phone booth and dialed the number that I still thought of as Russell Berger's. I needed to talk to Winnie again, to ask her about what it had been like for her to leave. Finally I had someone I could talk to about everything.

Even though there was nothing to be nervous about, my heart thudded as the phone rang. Winnie answered after two rings and told the operator she'd take the call. "I'm so glad you called. I've been thinking about you."

"I've been thinking about you too," I said.

"What've you been thinking?" Winnie asked.

"Just about your life. I mean, last time I was so . . . I didn't even ask what your life's like now."

"It's nice," Winnie answered. "Russ and I live in a small house just outside the city. We just moved, actually."

"What do you do? I mean, do you work?"

"I work for an advertising firm. Russ is in banking."

I couldn't believe this was my sister. She lived a Country life. No lying, no plotting, no stealing. Winnie never took off in the middle of the night. She never cringed when it rained, thinking of all the driveways and roofs bleeding black. She never had to go to sleep seeing the faces of the people she'd cheated. She'd left all that behind forever.

"How did you meet Russ, anyway?"

"He was on summer break from college, traveling the South with a few friends. They were staying at one of the campgrounds, and we got to know each other. For the rest of summer he followed us practically everywhere we went. We tried to keep it a secret from Dad, but he found out."

"I know you said Russ was why you left, but was that it?" I asked. "Was that the only reason? I mean, were you sad to leave?"

Winnie paused. "Sounds like Traveler life is getting you down."

"I don't know. I thought it was just marrying Patrick, but now I'm not so sure. He'd be a good husband—he'd be good to me, I know that."

"For me it was predominantly Russ," Winnie said.

The word *predominantly* stuck out to me. Winnie spoke differently than we did. If I kept going to school, I'd learn to speak that way too.

"But I also just wasn't sure I was cut out for Traveler life," she continued.

"I don't know if I am either," I admitted. "I didn't used to think I had a choice."

"You do." Winnie sighed like she wasn't so sure she should say what she was thinking. "Listen, sweetie, you could come stay with us for a little while if you want. Just take a break, try to figure things out."

I'd already thought about that. About leaving for good. About going to Winnie's. But now that she was offering, even if it'd just be for a little while to figure things out, my pulse quickened. "I don't know."

"Don't feel bad about that—about not knowing. You're right not to be sure about it."

"But how will I figure it out?" I asked.

"You just will," she said.

When I hung up, I didn't leave the booth right away. Right there in front of me was a phone book. Without thinking about it anymore, I riffled through it until I found the number for the bus station. I searched my pockets for a quarter, slid it into the slot, and dialed. My voice trembled as I asked for the schedule to Boston. The woman at the station told me that buses left twice a day every day, one at eight o'clock A.M. and one at four P.M.

Walking back across the campground, I noticed the backdrop of my life in a way I hadn't before. The trailers, parked this way and that—shiny new aluminum trailers, old rusty tin ones, huge RVs that had their own cabs, and SUVs pulling pop-up tent trailers—looked strange instead of familiar. What if I left and lived with Winnie for a while? What if my life was no longer black pavement, white lines, road signs, and guardrails? What if it wasn't tar and sealant and sweat? Maybe I'd start school in Boston and hang out with friends after school or even have them over to Winnie's. I'd say my parents had died in a car crash and Winnie had raised me. I could get another job like the one I had with Mrs. C. Maybe I would go on to college and study Roosevelt and Kennedy. It wouldn't be that hard to do. I'd leave a note and hitch to the station. Winnie could explain to Mom. Mom would still have Jimmy. Jimmy would keep in touch with me, and Mom would too. Dad wouldn't, but that would be the price I'd pay. I'd lose Patrick, and probably Ann. But there'd be so much more in my world. Wouldn't there?

It wasn't until a few days later that Jimmy and Patrick made it back. I was walking to the trailer after getting a Coke at the campground office and I found Jimmy sitting at the card table, drinking a beer. I broke into a jog and ran toward him.

"You're home!" I called out. I'd never been so excited to see him before. Because he'd made it back safely, but also because I'd just plain missed him.

Jimmy took a giant swig of beer and then plunked the bottle, empty except for a small lining of foam, on the table in front of him. "That I am."

I sat down across from him. His eyes were bloodshot, and a week's stubble covered his face.

"Where's Mom?" I asked. When I'd left to get the Coke, she'd been inside the trailer, and I was surprised she wasn't right there fussing all over Jimmy now that he was back.

"She went to the store to pick up stuff for dinner."

"Dad know you're back?"

Jimmy shook his head. "He should be here any second. Mom said he was washing the truck."

"Where's Patrick? Is he home too?"

"He was looking for you. I think he went to see his parents."

"He saved me, you know," I said.

Jimmy nodded. He picked up the beer bottle and tilted it in front of his face, looked at the foam sliding against the glass.

"What was it like being arrested?" I asked.

Jimmy shrugged, trying to be tough.

"Did they handcuff you and everything?"

"Yeah. Read me my rights. Stuck me in a cell and slammed the bars shut. Just like on TV."

"Shit," I breathed.

Jimmy made a face, again acting like it was no big deal, but I was pretty sure it was. It had to be. "So Mom said you talked to Winnie," he said.

I nodded. "I was so stupid for even thinking for a second Mom was having an affair."

Jimmy shrugged. "You had to think something."

"I also thought maybe it was about you—maybe you were in trouble."

Jimmy shook his head. "Me—trouble?" he chuckled.

I laughed with him and then said, "Winnie's nice, huh?"

Jimmy raised his gaze to mine. "I'm sorry I didn't tell you earlier. I thought it'd be best if you didn't know. I was older when she left. I couldn't just forget she'd ever existed, but you could."

"It's okay," I told him. "I understand."

Jimmy nodded and then said, "So I also hear we're having a wedding a little earlier than we thought. You come around to it?"

"Well, actually—" I paused and took a deep breath. Leaving was all I'd been thinking about. But of course I hadn't told anyone. The only person to tell would have been Ann, and I couldn't tell her because of Patrick. Jimmy would understand—he'd have to. And if I voiced my plan out loud I could see how it sounded, because in my mind it sounded good. "I've been thinking—"

I didn't get to finish my sentence because Dad pulled up in the truck, kicking up a swirl of dust. Jimmy and I looked away while the dust settled. Dad's shirt was wet from sweat and from washing the truck. "Look what the cat drug in," he said with a sneer as he lumbered toward us.

Jimmy muttered so that only I could hear him, "Good to see you too."

Dad started right in on him. Just the sight of Jimmy set him going. Maybe it was because Jimmy looked more and more like Big Jim every day—tall and thick. "You learn your lesson?" Dad asked.

"What lesson was I supposed to be learning?"

"You ready to settle down now? Stick to local jobs?"

I expected Jimmy's temper to flare like usual. For him to stand up and let fly. But instead he spoke calmly. "No." There was a sureness in his tone I'd never heard before. Like it didn't matter what Dad said—he'd made up his mind.

"Then we got a problem," Dad scoffed.

Jimmy's voice was still flat. "You don't have any problem. Once Big Jim gets off, I'm meeting up with him. I won't be a problem for you anymore."

My stomach seized up. Would Jimmy really leave? Or was he just baiting Dad? If he left, could I leave too? Could we do that to Mom and Dad? Leave them all alone?

"Jim's not getting off this time," Dad said, his voice rising. "He's got a rap sheet from his ass to his elbow. He's wanted in at least a half dozen states. He's not getting off. He's going to the *quad*."

Jimmy shook his head. "You don't know that."

"God, Jimmy, when are you gonna wake up?" Dad boomed. "I look at you and I can't believe I raised a fool for a son. Jim's life—that's no life. There's a reason our people have been doing the same thing for decades. For centuries. It's people like Jim who are ruining us. Can't you see that?"

Jimmy was still calm. He looked straight at Dad as he spoke. "Then that's people like me. Because I'm like Jim."

I wanted Jimmy to shout, to scream, to leap at Dad. Because the way he was talking, like nothing he said would make a difference, meant he'd given up caring.

"You know what?" Dad was seething. He looked down at the ground and toed the dirt with his work boot. It seemed as if he was making sure he really wanted to say what he was about to. I hoped he wouldn't—that somehow he'd keep his mouth shut—because I knew whatever came out would be far worse than any punch.

Dad looked back up at Jimmy and spoke with something in his eyes that looked more like hurt and sadness than anger. "You're right. You might as well be Jim's son, because you sure as hell ain't mine."

Dad turned and headed into the trailer. The screen door banged behind him. I heard him go into the bathroom and turn on the shower.

Jimmy said, "Well, I guess that settles that," but he wasn't so much talking to me as to himself. He stood up and started walking away.

"Wait," I called. "Where're you going?"

Jimmy waved, telling me to leave him be. I let him keep walking and sat at the card table, staring out at the dusty campground. I listened to Dad finish his shower, trudge into the kitchen, open the fridge for a beer, flip on the TV. It was the same old routine. It wouldn't ever change.

I was still there when Mom came back from the store. She could tell from my face that something wasn't right. She slid the bag of groceries onto the card table and looked around nervously. "Where's Jimmy?"

"I don't know. He left."

Mom's face dropped. "Left?"

"He just went somewhere."

"But he'll be back?" Mom's eyes danced and she fingered her throat.

"I guess so. I don't know. Dad said something to him."

"What'd he say?" Mom demanded.

When I didn't answer, Mom bolted into the trailer. Her voice was high-pitched, frantic. "What did you say to him?"

"Nothing that isn't the truth," Dad yelled over the blaring TV.

"I told you not to start with him," Mom cried. "I told you!"

"And I've told you I've had it with him. I don't care if we lose him. What good's he to this family anyway?"

"Douglas!" Mom pleaded.

"No," Dad said. "That's enough, Mary. Now goddamn it, let me sit in peace."

I waited for Mom to say something else, but she must've realized there was nothing left to say. Mom brought in good money from selling trailers and working Kmarts and Wal-Marts. She managed the finances and raised us kids. But Dad was the one who had the final say. Always. And that was the way it would be for me too.

Mom came back outside and eased into the chair across from me. She clasped my hand tight across the rickety old card table. "I can't lose him, Bridget," she whispered. "Not like I lost Winnie. I keep telling your father I can't lose another one of you, but he won't listen. He won't let Jimmy be." Mom squeezed my hand. "Go find him. Tell him I'm making his favorite—pork chops." Mom paused and then begged, "Please, Bridget, please."

"Okay," I said. "I'll go talk to him."

chapter 21

The blue sky was fading to the color of the smoking coals from people's grills when I found Jimmy in his truck. He'd taken his contact lenses out and he had his thick glasses on. I hadn't seen him in his glasses in years, and he looked both older and younger somehow. I went around to the passenger's side and climbed in. "Mom's making pork chops."

"I'm not going back," Jimmy said, his voice strong. "I'm leaving. Tonight. I don't even know why I came back."

"Dad didn't mean it about you not being his son," I tried to tell him. "And Mom—she'll die if you leave."

I readied myself to tell Jimmy what I'd started to before Dad had come home: that I was hoping to leave and go live with Winnie for a while. But he said, "You don't understand. I have to leave."

"I understand. I do. But Dad was just worked up. It's all this with Big Jim and—"

Jimmy cut me off, his tone desperate. "No, you *don't* understand. If I leave now, maybe I'll be able to see you guys sometimes down the road. Dad might forgive me for not marrying Ann, for going out on my own. But if I stay, I'll do something he won't forgive me for. I'll do something I won't forgive *myself* for."

"But Mom," I said. "You know how she loves you."

Jimmy swallowed. "I know. It's gonna be tough on her. But she has you and Patrick. That'll be enough."

I tried hard to hold back my tears, but a few rolled down my face. Jimmy reached out and brushed away one of my tears like he had that night in Belle Springs when I learned how he could be so strong and so gentle.

"You're gonna be all right," he whispered. "You all are."

"I don't know," I said.

"You'll be better off without me . . . without me driving y'all crazy."

Jimmy chuckled, but when he saw that I wasn't laughing he reached over and pulled me close. I couldn't remember the last time we'd hugged. We clutched each other, neither of us wanting to let go. Maybe because we knew that when we did, it'd never be the same again.

I stayed in the truck with Jimmy talking till past midnight. We watched the sun set and the moon rise, spreading its dim cloudy light, and remembered times growing up on the road, times before we were old enough to have the problems we did now, times that all kids had, not just Traveler kids. We laughed about racing our bikes around different campgrounds and always scraping our knees, about Dad winning watermelon seed–spitting contests, and about playing the license-plate game for ten cents a plate. Jimmy told me what he remembered about Winnie and when there had been five of us all together.

Instead of saying good-bye for real, Jimmy and I said we'd

see each other down the road. It just seemed easier that way. I wasn't sure when that'd be. A month. A year. Five years. Maybe not for a long, long time, depending on whether he was careful and whether he was lucky. He was wanted now—by the cops and by the bail bondsman.

Walking back to the trailer, I went by the Murphys', but no lights were on. No lights were on at our trailer either, and I didn't see Patrick sitting at the card table until I was a few feet from him.

"How long have you been waiting there?" I whispered.

"All night." Patrick stood up and took my hand. "Come on."

He led me behind the trailer, past a few more trailers to the edge of a field filled with honeysuckle. He'd been there earlier, and there was a blanket on the ground. Patrick brought me to the blanket and got down on one knee.

"What are you doing?"

"I never asked you, and I think it's only right," he said. "But first I want to tell you something. What I was gonna tell you before we were arrested." Patrick trained his eyes on me and spoke clearly. "I wanted to with you, more than you know. But I love you, and I didn't want to risk losing you for something that was worth making myself wait for. It wasn't about the bride-price. It was about not losing you."

I knelt down so I was facing Patrick. He kissed me, carefully at first, like he was testing if I wanted him to, and I answered by kissing him back.

"I want to tonight," he breathed between kisses. "I want to with you."

"You'll have to show me," I said, glad he couldn't see me turn red in the dim light of the moon and the stars.

Patrick shook his head. "No, I can't."

There was something in the way he looked at me—like he was embarrassed and somehow proud at the same time. "We'll have to figure it out together," he said shyly.

"You mean you never—" I stopped myself, sure he had.

Patrick shook his head again and whispered, "No."

"But I heard you and Jimmy talking."

"I just messed around a little. I never did it with any of them." He took my hand and held it tight. "Bridget, will you marry me?"

I looked into Patrick's pale blue eyes. After everything, all my worrying and crying, he'd been waiting so it could be the two of us together. I couldn't blame him for fooling around a little—out of desire, out of curiosity, out of the fact that he was only eighteen and about to promise himself to one woman for the rest of his life. I'd have done the same thing if I'd had the chance, if it was different for Traveler girls. But he'd saved himself for me, and I believed he'd be true to me. I wanted to thank him, but I didn't exactly think I could thank him for that. Then I remembered I hadn't yet thanked him for what he did back in Arizona.

"Thank you for saving me," I said.

"Stay out here with me tonight," he whispered.

Patrick was back in my heart—this time I hoped for good.

"I'll stay," I said.

And I would. I would stay.

author's note

As with so much in life, sometimes the best things happen by complete co-incidence. Or maybe it's fate, depending on what you want to believe. For me, stumbling on the Travelers was both. I first learned about the Travelers by randomly picking up a newspaper that featured an article on them. Their unique culture immediately fascinated me. I cut out the article and tucked it away in my file of possible story ideas. But unlike many articles, jotted notes, photographs, and ticket stubs collected over the years, the Travelers kept popping into my head. I knew I would find a story to write about them.

Because the Travelers mostly keep to themselves and stay just under the radar screen, there's not that much information easily available on them. I read what few nonfiction books and articles I could find to gain a sense of their lives and issues, but when I started writing, characters like Bridget, Jimmy, Patrick, Ann, and Big Jim took on a life of their own.

While the Travelers certainly do exist, and many of the rules, traditions, and events described in *See You Down the Road* are based on the accounts I read about the Travelers, the story and characters are purely fictional. Like any culture, Travelers include a wide range of people, behaviors, attitudes, and preferences. The Daughertys and Murphys in no way represent all Travelers. If anything, they are a product of my imagination and a reflection of my interests.

Many people helped me along the way, and I would like to acknowledge their contributions to this story. Thanks to my family, especially Mom and Dad for their unwavering encouragement of all my various ventures, Grandma and Grandpa for their continued support, and Matt, Brisby, and Spruce for always being there for me. Also thanks to Jenny Belknap for countless conversations about Bridget's choices, Bill Holinger for always knowing just what needs to be done, Jeff Dwyer and Elizabeth O'Grady for believing in me, Nancy Hinkel for loving the characters as much as I do and for expert editorial guidance, the reader from the Traveler community for adding his insight and experience, copy editor Artie Bennett and his crew for their wonderful attention to detail, art designer Melissa Nelson for realizing my dream vision of the cover and book design, and Lara Zeises for last-minute consultation. I am also grateful to the PEN New England Children's Book Caucus, who chose this book for their 2002 Discovery Award. *See You Down the Road* would also not have been possible without the generous Work-in-Progress Grant for a Contemporary Novel for Young People from the Society of Children's Book Writers and Illustrators, sponsored by Judy Blume. Finally, a sadly-too-late thanks to Morse Hamilton—the first writer and teacher to believe in my writing.